LOCKDOWN FEMINIZATION

1

Feminized and turned into a sissy maid through humiliation and submission

Lady Alexa

Copyright © Lady Alexa 2020

All rights reserved. No reproduction, copy or transmission of this publication or section in this publication may be reproduced copied or transmitted without written permission of the author.

This novel is a work of fiction. Names, characters, businesses, places, events and incidents are either the products of the author's imagination or used in a fictitious manner. Any resemblance to actual persons, living or dead, or actual events is purely coincidental.

This novel contains explicit scenes of a sexual nature including forced male to female gender transformation, female domination, humiliation, CFNM, spanking and reluctant feminisation. All characters in this story are aged 18 and over.

Strictly for adults aged 18 and over or the age of maturity in your country.

Subscribe to my newsletter and receive discounts and offers on forced-feminisation stories and sex toys.

Enrol from my blog at:

www.ladyalexauk.com

CONTENTS

Chapter 1 – All Change

Chapter 2 – Lady Luck Smiles

Chapter 3 – The World is Full of Bossy Women

Chapter 4 – The Journey Begins

Chapter 5 – Nowhere-Ville

Chapter 6 – A Feminine World

Chapter 7 – A Fluffy Gown

Chapter 8 – A Change of Clothing

Chapter 9 – Enemy Contact

Chapter 10 – House Rules

Chapter 11 – A Skirt is No Joke

Chapter 12 – Housework Time

Chapter 13 – A Pretty Sissy

Chapter 14 – Babydolls and Panties

Chapter 15 – Trouble With a Capital E

Chapter 16 – Shrinking Masculinity

Chapter 17 – Clothes Make the Girl

Chapter 18 – Happy in Skirts

Chapter 19 – Shaved and Smooth

Chapter 20 – Damp Patches

Chapter 21 – Accustomed to Femininity

Chapter 22 – Disguised as a Girl

Chapter 23 – Accentuate the Femininity

Chapter 24 – The Feminine Exhibit

Chapter 25 – Never Too Girly

Chapter 26 – Meeting the Mistress

Chapter 27 – She Wants a Sissy Too

Chapter 28 – Curtsey Sissy

Chapter 1 — All Change

David Amey was at home watching evening TV when he lost his job. His boss dismissed him by text message. It was 9 pm exactly and the manner of his dismissal made it all the more annoying.

He had been working as a personal assistant for the high-flyer Chicago lawyer, Anne Dufort. He didn't have a contract; it was cash in hand. And how he needed that cash. London was not a cheap place to survive for a thirty-five-year-old man with no qualifications or any obvious skills, aside from an inherent ability to follow orders from bossy women without complaint.

David slammed the mobile phone on the coffee table, the screen still lit with her message.

It lay there with the offending message, next to three empty cans of beer and a foil container crusting with the dried remains of an earlier microwave curry. What he called a coffee table was made of chipboard and covered with a peeling white veneer. He had found it dumped in the street by the recycling bins a few weeks ago.

The TV in the corner of the small room showed a newsreader with over-styled hair that had seen too much hairspray was on the screen. She described the efforts of the government to contain a new virus spreading around the globe. A possible pandemic, she said, adding that for now the government was not imposing any lockdown. They were aiming for herd immunity. An expert explained to the newsreader on a split-screen that they planned for people to catch the virus and therefore become immune. She said they may have to change the approach and predicted a lockdown was coming very soon.

David slumped back into the sofa, a loose spring cut into his back. *Great,* he thought, *not only no job but soon no freedom either. Could this evening get any worse?*

Chapter 2 — Lady Luck Smiles

David ran his fingers through his long blond hair, a reminder of his now ex-boss's rules. It was a condition of the job. She had disapproved of his cropped greying hair when he first started the job, nearly two years ago.

"I don't want my personal assistant looking like an ageing ex-marine," she used to say.

This was a massive exaggeration, Anne Dufort was prone to that. He was far too scrawny to look anything like a serviceman. Everything for her was always *awesome or amazing*. She insisted he use her hairdresser once a month, she said she wanted his hair *awesome* and *amazing*. He liked the attention he got at the salon, and from her. He was less keen on the feminine style they gave him. There was something that niggled at him about his hair, something *interesting* about it. More than once she had caught him stroking it with affection. It felt nice.

He was always the only man at Ms Dufort's hair salon. After two years in her employment, he had shoulder-length hair, coloured ash-blond. She had said it was similar to the grey-mousey colour he used to have. He wasn't sure this was entirely true.

He thought about the comments he used to get.

"Can I help you miss? Oh, I'm sorry, I mean sir. Excuse me miss. Oh, I'm sorry, you're a sir."

Very funny, he had heard these comments a few times. No, a thousand times. Now he could get it all cut off and there would be no more comments. He would get no more salary either.

He inspected the nails of his hand, they were clean and shaped. Too long to be masculine, not long enough to be feminine. Anne Dufort wanted him clean, tidy and well-dressed. He liked her for that, he wanted to be tidy. The problem was it was too much effort without her pushing him into it. And push she had.

She had also dressed him in expensive business suits. He thought them a little too fitted, but high quality nonetheless. Anne Dufort moved in senior circles: politicians, business people and the like. She told him she didn't want her *personal assistant* to be wearing untidy trainers. Or as she called them, *sneakers*. She didn't want him to have bitten-down nails. Or a military haircut. And then there was the sitting. She had taught him to be graceful, legs together when he sat.

Personal assistant, a grand name for what he did for her. Personal serf might have been a better title.

He glared at the news on the TV. It was miserable, to match his mood. Shots of hospital wards across Europe showed things were getting out of hand. The virus was affecting thousands. A doctor in a white medical coat was being interviewed live from a major hospital. She said the Government needed to reverse its policy of waiting for herd immunity and impose restrictions now. If they didn't, things were going to get worse. She demanded a lockdown.

He didn't want this bad news on top of his dismissal; he was becoming depressed. He cursed and looked up in frustration. The ceiling was stained yellow from the cigarette fumes of the previous tenant. The faint odour of stale smoke from the previous tenant lingered through the smell of stale curry from its current occupant.

His once-white trainers beat an urgent anxious rhythm on the plastic laminate flooring. The cheap covering curled up at the joins. A top-of-the-range logo blared from his sports shoes. He had bought them from a street trader in east London at a fraction of the shop price two weeks ago. The soles were coming away and he ruminated on how that goes to show even the best brands are not made to last these days.

He leant forward and slapped his forehead in the palms of his hands in frustration. His fingers laced into his long fringe or as Anne Dufort had called it, his *bangs*. His fringe touched against thin, plucked eyebrows. Another one of her little requirements. He sat still for a moment on the sofa, knees together to one side. Like Anne Dufort had taught him. It was natural now, he never realised.

Now what was he going to do? His rent was three months in arrears and he had no savings. It wasn't as if she paid him a lot of money. It was enough to get by though; it wasn't as if it was taxed.

His cracked mobile phone screen was still lit from Anne Dufort's dismissal text message. She, of course, had another name for his phone: a *cell*.

Wasn't that a prison or something, he thought? Why would she call it a cell? He didn't know. He didn't care.

Another ping sounded. He jumped. A second text had arrived from his ex-boss. He snatched at the phone, his lip and one cheek curling. On cue, the TV screen showed graphs with dire predictions of a surge in UK Coronavirus cases. He looked away and back down at his mobile phone. *Cellphone.* He opened the text message as he scratched at the day-old stubble on his chin. The message was much longer than her curt dismissal message. He peered at it through the fissures on the screen glass.

"Amy, I've been offered a partnership at my law company in the States at short notice. I've recommended you to my friend, Fiona. She's

been looking for someone to work for her as a personal assistant for ages without luck. She needs someone who does whatever they are told. Like you. I took the liberty of passing her your cell number. She'll contact you. Goodbye."

He shuddered, not sure if it was the cold in the apartment or her irritating habit of calling him by his last name. And misspelling it Amy instead of Amey. She called most people by their surname, but most people didn't have a feminine sounding surname. She called the concierge Smith, her secretary in Chicago Haswell and her accountant Myerscough. David's surname was ambiguous, it sounded like a girl's name. Especially as she never spelt it correctly.

For, two years, he endured the sniggers of her calling him Amy in public. Added to his hairstyle, and nails, it was humiliating. He needed the money so he endured it with a scowl. And he found his boss and her strange ways oddly exciting. It was more than the money. He wasn't sure exactly what it was he found exciting working for her. There was something and it was not only about her being sexy. His memories stirred a while.

He thought about getting another sweater. He couldn't afford to put on the electric heaters. It was spring, but spring in London can be warm or cold. This year it was cold and wet; the rain splattered on his fifteenth-floor apartment windows. The plain scuffed magnolia walls had dark marks around the skirting board. Suspicious black patches grew by the ceiling.

They had become larger over the past couple of months.

The TV newsreader was still droning on about Coronavirus; he wanted good news. He was fed up with it, but the batteries in the remote were dead and he couldn't be bothered to get up to switch it off.

Another ping sounded from his phone, he had never had so many texts in one night. Not since he had been dating the healthcare worker, Olga. She did massages at a Health Centre somewhere, she was never clear which one. He remembered she was Russian, or Ukrainian or something. Many Bulgarian or Rumanian? She never said. She had dry bleached hair, dark black eyeshadow and a pale face. He wondered if he would bump into her at the local health centre one day if he had the need to see a doctor. She also did home visits, which was nice of her. He thought about her for a while. They had split up over the rash she had given him. She told him she must have caught it off a patient and then touched herself by accident.

He picked his phone up.

The message read, *"Hello Amy, my name is Fiona Ryder. Anne Dufort passed me your number. She has recommended you as a personal assistant. Let me know whether know you're available for an interview. If so, I'll send you my address."*

David grinned to himself. Maybe Lady Luck was smiling on him after all.

Chapter 3 — The World is Full of Bossy Women

Fiona Ryder? The name was familiar. She was a celebrity of some kind, a journalist or writer? He wasn't sure, maybe someone with the same name. Besides, he didn't read books or newspapers, he considered them boring, for boring people. He was sure someone called Fiona Ryder had been on TV a few times. He peered at her message again and sniggered. Even she couldn't spell his surname right, weren't writers supposed to be good at spelling, he thought?

He perked up at the possibility of falling into another job, it was all going to be alright after all. A friend of Anne Dufort's? He hoped this Fiona woman wouldn't want him with a sissy hairstyle, shaped nails and plucked eyebrows. He tucked his hair behind one ear and pressed reply. His fingernail shone under the ceiling bulb hanging bare above his head.

He typed, *"Hi Fiona Im intrestid in the work Im free eny time."*

He pressed send with a buzz of excitement zinging across his chest.

The reply came back within seconds.

"Good. Be here sharp tomorrow, 5 pm. My address is the Old Farm House, Green Lane, Theydon Bisset, Berkshire. Postcode, TB97 2XX. I hope you are as reliable and compliant as Anne says. The post is for a live-in assistant. I haven't been able to find anyone suitable and

I'm on a tight deadline to complete my latest novel. Don't be late."

David stared at the screen with disbelief. Did he have a guardian angel looking after him? Anne Dufort must have thought him a good worker to do this for him: a recommendation. What a stroke of luck. But where the hell was Theydon Bisset, he wondered? What kind of name was that?

He googled Theydon Bisset on his phone after checking the spelling several times. It didn't look good: the images showed stone cottages, a village pub and lots of fields. This place was a quiet traditional English village in the countryside, some 60 miles west of London. *Nowhere-Ville,* he thought. Nearest station:

Newbury. Where the hell was Newbury? The backside of nowhere, that's for sure.

He read on. He would have to get a taxi or a bus twelve miles from Newbury station to the village. He googled the postcode and his body slumped. The Old Farm House was an isolated house, three miles outside Theydon Bisset. He didn't have a lot of choice, there was no other work. Besides, it was too much effort to search for one.

He then googled Fiona Ryder. It changed the search term to F L Ryder, the pen name for Fiona Ryder. Her images filled the screen. If this was the same person then this was going to be a good job. She was attractive in a mature lady way. It said she was forty-five. She was slim with flowing silver hair. She looked like an actress. He rubbed his hands together.

Filled with a renewed enthusiasm, he typed back, *"Hi Fiona Ill be their tomorroe at 5 sharp thanks."*

He pressed send and it swished away into the web. He added Fiona Ryder's number to his contact list.

He decided it was time for bed, now he felt able to sleep after all. He put the phone in his pocket and floated over to the TV. He waited a moment as images of patients in rows of hospital beds filled the screen. A breaking newsflash rolled across the bottom of the screen: The Government were meeting in the evening to discuss a country-wide lockdown within twenty-four hours. He flicked the TV off. It was depressing.

He plodded to his bed at the opposite end of the room. The bed-covers were half on and half off the single mattress, creased and yellowing. He stretched, yawned and undressed before slumping onto the bed. He pulled up the covers, sliding naked into the cold, damp sheets. He shivered and reached out to place his phone on the old pine bedside table. A drawer front was hanging off where the screws needed tightening. The phone pinged again. He grimaced and leant out to pick up the phone.

The name Fiona Ryder was on the message header. He opened the text. *"You'll address me as Ms Ryder, Amy."*

"Oh no, another arrogant bitch," he said to himself. "Whatever."

He put the phone back on the bedside unit and fell asleep in an instant.

Chapter 4 — The Journey Begins

He woke with a start and grabbed his phone. 11.03 am showed through the cracks on the screen. Today was his big day. A new job opportunity. If Anne Dufort had taught him one thing, it was to give himself time. *Contingency*, she had called it. He still didn't know exactly what that meant. He supposed he could have looked it up online but that was too much effort and anyway, he'd forget again so there was no point.

He jumped out of bed. He showered, shaved and put on the suit and shirt Anne Dufort had bought him to wear. After a breakfast of bread and jam, he left his apartment. He closed the front door, the click echoed around the cold fluorescent-lit passageway.

A chill blew down the hallway and bit against his face. A window was open in the stairwell at the end of the passage. An intermittent buzzing sounded from a strip light overhead; it had flickered as if about to give out for the past three months. He strode to the lifts and pressed the down button. He thought for a moment, what was it Dufort called them? *Elevators*. Yes. She had a different word for everything, it seemed.

He waited for several minutes. No lift arrived. Out of order again. The council spent most of its finances and energy on the new apartments on the other side of the borough. The places for the rich. He took the stairs, he had plenty of time. *Contingency.*

The tube station, or what Ms Dufort called the *subway station*, was at the end of the road. He took the underground train to Paddington Station, in the west of the city. He bought a day-return from the miserable lady at the ticket office and passed through the barrier. He found an empty carriage and settled down for the forty-five-minute journey to Newbury. The train pulled out; Lady Luck was definitely smiling on him.

Chapter 5 — Nowhere-Ville

He didn't know what to do on the journey. What can you do when there's no TV? Probably just as well, he thought, the only story was the virus. Surely something else was going on in the world?

A young lady came through the inter-connecting carriage doors and sat down on the other side of the aisle, next to the window. She had white earphones in and was switching on a Kindle. She placed the Kindle face up on the seat next to her and fiddled with her mobile phone. She scrolled through songs on her screen. The Kindle screen caught his eye, it had a book cover with a colour image of an attractive woman with long legs and a sexy mini skirt. The title read, *Feminized and Pretty 1 by Lady Alexa.* That was a strange title and author name. An English aristocrat writing a novel, whatever next?

He picked up an abandoned free newspaper from the seat facing him. The headlines screamed about the growing pandemic. Yawning, he turned to the back pages, sport was more interesting than all this hysteria. Instead, he saw more dramatic headlines about the virus. Several sports stars had contracted the virus and the government were considering closing down all live sports events. He threw the newspaper across the carriage. The young lady looked across at him.

Forty-five minutes later, he arrived at Newbury station, bored. He didn't have enough cash for a taxi from Newbury, he hadn't realised how much the train fare would be. He found the bus station and caught a bus to Theydon Bisset. Luckily he had *contingency*. Lots of time. He silently thanked Anne Dufort for teaching him this idea. He wondered if he should have taught her how to spell his name correctly. She wouldn't have liked him to correct her, e had probably made the right decision to let it be.

A long slow journey ensued. He felt as if they stopped at every bus stop on the way. Finally he arrived at the village; it was the end of the route. He got up and walked to the front of the bus and asked the driver when the next bus to the Old Farm House would be. The driver said nothing for a moment. Then she laughed.

Her eyes ran over his hairstyle and fitted suit. Her thin smile was unfriendly. "No buses run into the countryside, you're not in London now," said, picking up on David's accent.

David got off the bus and looked around. The village had a single high street, 600 yards long. A white-washed pub advertised local ales on white chalk writing on a black board, a newsagent was closing. Either side of the street, grey-stone Edwardian and Victorian cottages lined up like soldiers at attention. A red telephone booth outside the newsagents was empty, the phone equipment long since removed.

He was going to have to walk to Fiona Ryder's house. He cast an eye up at the heavy clouds. It was late March and the start of spring, but the air was damp and the light was as grey as the village buildings. He pulled his collars up on the thin suit jacket, he wished he had been able to afford a coat.

If only he had had some luck at the bookies. No chance, his horses never seemed to win. His suit tugged taut across his body, the jacket gathered in at the waist. It had two large buttons at the front. He guessed it was the current style, he didn't keep up with those things. The creases on his trousers were falling out, he had forgotten to press them and the long journey and damp air hadn't helped. There was no Anne Dufort to remind him. Never mind, he thought, at least he had a suit to wear for the interview.

He set off out of the village, phone in hand showing him the way. He walked out on a narrow road, lined with low stone walls, and into the countryside. Soon there were no buildings, just fields and trees.

Rain continued to threaten, thick wetness hung in the air. The first spits started falling as he started the last mile of the three-mile walk. The clouds opened and torrential rain fell on him as if someone was tipping buckets of water over him. The rain bounced off the tarmac road like tiny dancers. He hunkered his shoulders and slugged along, hoping for a vehicle to pass. None came, even the fields were deserted. After another twenty miserable minutes walking through the curtain of rain, he arrived at a wide wooden barred gate. He was cold, unhappy and drenched, the once vague trouser creases a distant memory.

The gate was set between two stone posts. A gravel drive stretched out for 200 yards to a farmhouse style house, made of the grey stone. There was no colour anywhere, even the fields and trees were a grey-green shade. A black metal sign with white engraved text was fixed on one post: The Old Farmhouse. He had arrived. He pulled his phone from a soaked pocket: 4.55 pm and an hour to sunset. In the deep gloom, it seemed as if the sun had already left for the evening. He was in time though, and this was the most important thing. He lifted the latch on the gate and went through.

He walked up the driveway, his feet squelching underfoot on the puddles in the gravel. It felt as if he had a pint of water in each shoe. He arrived at a black panelled front door and stood on the raised doorstep. It was under a small canopy. At that moment, the rain stopped. The soaked suit was stuck to him like a sheet of icy-cold cling film and he was drenched through to his underpants. His once styled long hair lay flat over his head and shoulders, like a long stringy cap. He saw no knocker or bell so rapped on the glossy front door with the back of his knuckles. His leg muscles ached; it had been many years since he had walked so far. Since he had walked anywhere.

He looked around. A dank smell of manure and wet leaves hung around him below the low angry clouds. He was at the only building on a country lane amongst a sea of fields and small copses. If Fiona Ryder wanted isolation, she had it here.

He stamped his feet to try to keep warm as a bitter wind started up. Water oozed out of the soles. He waited several minutes before the front door swung open. A woman appeared, her face creased in surprise. David recognised her immediately from the online photos, Fiona Ryder, F L Ryder the writer. She was more attractive in the flesh than in the online photos. Her hair was silver-blond and she radiated health in the way wealthy people managed. Her face was too smooth and unlined for someone in their mid-forties, the only creases were tiny laughter lines around her eyes. She was taller than David, even in flat shoes. Her body was slim and lithe and clad in skin-tight blue jeans. He thought of her as looking like a female cheetah, an effect accentuated by her leopard-skin style top. The top buttons were undone, revealing two generous mounds of round tight breast.

She stood for a moment taking in his bedraggled appearance. "Yes?" she said, not comprehending why a dishevelled man was standing at her front door in the middle of nowhere.

"I'm David," he said, wiping the water from his eyes, it ran from his drenched fringe, which was stuck to his forehead.

She looked him up and down a couple of times. She put one of her arms went across the doorway as if preventing him from rushing in. Her movement was deliberate and athletic like a gymnast.

"OK, and what is it I can do for you, David?" Her eyes were cool and flowed over him again.

"If you're a reporter who's come out here to interview me or a salesman you've had a wasted journey. And you got wet for nothing."

Was this some kind of joke? What was going on?

"You are Ms Ryder? F L Ryder?" David asked as he shivered and dripped water onto the step.

"I see. You're a reporter trying to get a story. You can forget it. Contact my agent."

She stepped back and started to close the door on him.

David was startled, confused. He had travelled miles, spent all his money and now she didn't know anything about their arrangement. He shivered.

"I've come for the job interview, Ms Ryder. Anne Dufort suggested me to you. You sent me a text. You asked me to come here. Here I am."

Her expression remained confused for a long moment. Then her eyes widened as the realisation filtered into her brain. The door remained half closed.

"The interview was for a young lady called Amy. Who are you? How do you know I have a job?" Her voice was now less sure. "This is a scam. Go away, young man."

She went to close the door. Had he come all this way for nothing?

Chapter 6 — A Feminine World

He put a hand to the door to stop her from closing it. He cleared his throat. "I'm Amey. David Amey."

She stopped. He put out a wet hand to shake hers. She stared hard into his blinking eyes. She shook her head. Then realisation flooded into her eyes.

"But Anne said you were called Amy. She never said you were *David* Amey. Are you telling me you're a man?" She put a hand across her forehead.

David shivered again. "Yes, Ms Dufort called me by my surname. It was her way. I'm David Amey, A M E Y."

Ms Ryder took in his bedraggled appearance. Her face softened.

"I'm so sorry, David. My poor manners, I was shocked you weren't a girl. Whatever, you need to come in and get dried and change out of those clothes. We can sort out the misunderstanding later. Let's get you warm and dry first. If Anne says you're OK, then you're OK."

She ushered him in and stepped away and he walked past her into the hallway. Her sweet floral perfume caught his nose with an underlying scent of freshly washed clothes.

The warmth of her hallway enveloped him like a cosy blanket. His clothes steamed. She shut the door on the wind and grey skies and he was ensconced in a world of femininity. Pink floral wallpaper covered the walls, an uplighter threw a warm yellow glow in the daytime gloom through a tasselled lampshade. Fiona's hair glistened in the light.

"I suggest you get yourself upstairs and take a shower," she said. "And while you're doing that, I'll fix you a hot drink and something to eat for when you're done. It's a long way from London, especially in this weather." A kind smile hovered on her smooth face. A hint of shine on her skin. "Then once you're warmed up, we can talk about this...," she thought for a moment. "This misunderstanding." She looked him over again. "Take your shoes and socks off, David, you're making a puddle."

He removed his drenched shoes and socks then held up a shoe to look more closely. The sole was peeling away; they hadn't survived the intense downpour. He stood in his bare feet and shivered one long shudder. Drips continued to fall from his suit and hair, splatting onto the tiled hallway floor around him.

"Your clothes are drenched. You need to get out of them and into the shower. I'll show you up to the spare bedroom where there's a private en-suite shower. The bedroom I allocated for..." She hesitated. "For my new live-in personal assistant." She thought for a moment. "I'll find you one of my dressing gowns while I hang your clothes up to dry. We're more or less the same size, maybe you're a bit smaller." She chuckled and thought for an instant. "Anne told me Amy was sensitive and effeminate, but I assumed she meant you were a girly girl. I didn't understand what she meant. Until now." Her eyes widened.

His body stiffened. Effeminate? He looked down ashamed.

"Ms Ryder, it's Amey with an *e* and it's my surname. My name is David."

"Yes, so you said." Fiona Ryder looked amused.

Fiona Ryder was not at all like her friend Anne 'Snooty' Dufort, he wondered how Fiona Ryder and Anne Dufort could ever be friends. Ms Ryder's kindly nature was what he needed right now.

David shook off her unintended slight. "Thank you, Ms Ryder, I'd like to get showered and to warm up."

"Excellent. Get your clothes off and you can follow me upstairs."

He shivered again. "Excuse me."

Had he heard right? Had she told him to take his clothes off? He guessed he had misunderstood and waited for her to repeat what she meant.

"You can't go dripping up the stairs. You'll ruin the carpet, it cost me a fortune. So, remove your clothes and then you can follow me to the shower." She folded her arms across her chest.

He hadn't misunderstood, she expected him to strip off naked. She didn't seem to think this was an odd request.

He waited, unsure what to do. "Er, er," he stuttered. "Couldn't you get your gown and then you can turn your back while I change.

She tapped a foot. "Come on David, you don't have anything I haven't seen before, I'm sure." Impatience crept into her voice. There was an edge to her after all. Her carpet was clearly more important than his self-esteem.

He looked up the carpeted stairs. She had a point, the carpet looked expensive and he didn't want to ruin it. He shivered again as she indicated he hurry up with a wave of one hand. She was being practical, he realised and shrugged. It could be worse, he thought, and peeled off his jacket, jumper and shirt. He was now naked from the waist up, the warmth from the radiator brushing over him.

She appraised his skinny hairless chest and slim arms without interest. Her hands remained folded across her breasts, she was waiting and they were going nowhere until he did what she had asked. He undid his belt and trouser button and pulled the zip down. His soaked trousers fell around his ankles as if they had a heavy weight attached. A damp puddle formed around his feet. He stepped out of the trousers and stood shivering in clinging wet underpants. They were stuck to his skin, wrapped around a shrunken penis and balls like a second skin. Her eyes flitted momentarily to his small bulge, her eyebrows lifted.

"You're going to catch pneumonia if you stand there all wet, young man. You'll get chilly in your willy." She laughed for an instant at her joke. "Take your underpants off, David. They are dripping wet too." Her face had a sparkle of amusement on it. "You're not going anywhere in dripping clothes. Underpants. Off. Now."

She clapped once which made him jump. It was strip off or stay there all day. He breathed in and pulled his underpants down and stepped out of them. His penis was small and shrivelled by the ice-cold rainwater, his balls had retreated into his body. He pulled both hands over his cold shrunken genitals. She looked at them and her nose wrinkled. She kept her eyes down there for a moment too long to be comfortable for David.

"Better," she said. "Now follow me upstairs. When you've finished, you can come back down and meet me in the kitchen. I'll wait for you there." She turned towards the stairs to her right.

She pointed to an open door off the hall on her right. He could see a double-range cooker, beyond the kitchen door. There was a row of glossy-fronted white kitchen units. His hands remained over his cold shrivelled penis, his knees bent together.

"I need to think about what I'm going to do with you." She shook her head. "You not being the female I expected. Or wanted."

She moved towards the stairs and glanced back over a shoulder. She wagged an index finger for him to follow. He followed her up the stairs to the next floor, Fiona Ryder's long silver hair bobbed as she walked. He caught another scent as he followed her; fresh shampoo. He watched the slight sway of her bottom in the tight blue jeans. With her back to him, he let his hands drop away, putting one on the bannister to steady himself. She turned into a second set of stairs from the landing which led up to the next floor. She glanced back and down at his cold shrivelled penis. She puckered her nose as if to say, *how cute*. He flushed red.

Wooden slatted steps led into a conversion in the roof space. There was a door at the top which opened into a light airy room. Two windows followed the drop of the roof at the front. At the back of the room, there was a large dormer that had patio-style doors the entire length. He saw the dark clouds clearing beyond them.

He walked into the bedroom following behind Fiona. Fiona Ryder's feminine style was evident all over the room: lacy curtains with light purple-flowered wallpaper. The bed-covers on the queen-sized bed were powder pink with white frills. A cream rug covered the light oak floorboards next to the bed.

"My personal assistant's room. When I find her."

His face dropped at her words.

"I prefer my employees and co-workers to be female. I find it a more inclusive environment. Men can be so competitive and aggressive. False machismo will enter a working environment when there's a male involved." She spoke matter-of-factly.

He felt he was now intruding in her female environment. This wasn't going to end well, he thought.

"The shower room is behind the door." She pointed to the far corner of the room. "I'll leave the dressing gown on the bed while you're showering."

She left the bedroom and glanced back one more time and down at his shrunken penis. He thought he saw a glint of amusement in her eyes again. He heard her stepping down the stairs.

The heating in the room was on full. His body was thawing out and drying. He walked naked to the dormer doors. The sound of regular drips of water came from somewhere outside. A watery sun glistened through clearing clouds. Typical, he thought, it only rained when he was walking from the village. Now it's stopped.

He cursed his bad luck and the bad luck that she wanted a female assistant. Lady Luck had not been there for him after all. He guessed she was going to send him back to London, judging by her comments. There would be no job for him here, she had been clear.

He went into the shower room in the corner and twisted the shower tap on full. He scrubbed and soaked under the hot water. Steam filled the small room. He poured shampoo over his head. He scrubbed his long thick hair, down his neck and around the top of his narrow shoulders. He ran the soap around his genitals, relieved they were returning to their normal size. Not big, he had to admit, but better than when Ms Ryder had seen them. What an embarrassment.

He finished washing and rinsing and felt refreshed. Now it was time to go back downstairs to see Ms Ryder; to face the situation he now found himself in. She had been clear, she wanted a female household. He turned the shower off and stepped out of the glass cubicle onto a thick pink floor towel. He grabbed a large red towel hanging on a chrome heated rail. It was warm and soft. It felt like he was in a hotel.

He left the shower room and stared out of the patio-door windows, the towel wrapped around his shoulders. The Old Farm House was exactly as the name had indicated. From the outside, he had seen it was like a postcard picture of a typical English farmhouse. From the top-floor windows, he saw it was surrounded on three sides by a six-foot-high wooden fence. It backed onto open farmland. The back garden was around 90 yards long, with a lawn and three old apple trees. Flower beds lined the edges.

He noticed a figure in the garden, looking up at him. He couldn't make out if it was a man or a woman. The person was stocky and dressed in trousers, green boots and a dark jacket. He stepped away from the windows.

Inside, he had seen the house was modern with everything being of obvious high quality. Someone had renovated it recently. He guessed it had been Ms Ryder.

How he would love to live here and be Fiona Ryder's assistant. He shook his head. It wasn't going to happen. It was time to go downstairs and face his fate.

Chapter 7 — A Fluffy Gown

A white towel dressing gown lay on the bed, as Fiona had promised. She had placed two white slippers at the foot of the queen-sized bed. He hadn't heard Ms Ryder come into his room over the noise of the shower. The feeling of being in a hotel returned.

He felt better, warmer, but sad. Fiona Ryder had expected a female, the job was not his. He sat on the end of the bed and sank into the soft mattress. He put his legs to one side, knees tight together. He would love to live and work her, instead, he had a problem: no money, no job and miles from home. This situation was worse than before he had left London.

He knew he couldn't mope around, although this is what he wanted to do. He had to go downstairs and face Fiona Ryder and his future. He picked up the dressing gown and put it on. He couldn't find the inner ties at first then realised it was because the gown was the other way round. The girl's side. Of course it was, it belonged to Ms Ryder. He re-wrapped the soft gown around himself and did up the internal ties. He tied the belt tight around his thin waist.

The gown was shorter than mid-thigh, shorter than he was comfortable with. He had no underwear on. He hoped Fiona Ryder was hanging his clothes up to dry. The end of his flaccid penis was only an inch or so from the hem of the gown. He had no choice, Ms Ryder had provided what she could. She had done her best for him.

He pushed his feet into the fluffy white slip-on slippers and left the bedroom. His spindly legs were white and exposed. He clattered down the stairs, the soles of the slippers clacking on the bare wooden steps of the top flight. His penis swung left and right beneath the gown; he enjoyed how it felt rubbing against the soft woollen material. A tingle fizzed in the end. He did not want it to get hard, it might show below the short hem of the gown. It was one thing to strip off for practical reasons, quite another to be seen with an erection.

He went down the next flight and into the hall and through to the kitchen at the back of the house. He tried to ignore the feeling of his warm penis swinging free an inch from exposure. Ms Ryder was sat at a pine kitchen table, sipping on a white mug of tea. She wore a pair of reading glasses she hadn't been wearing before. She was concentrating on printed pages scattered around her, scribbling and crossing out with a small pencil.

On the black granite kitchen worktop, there was an old-fashioned style radio. He saw it was a modern digital radio in the design of a 1950s radio. A voice-over from the radio announced he was listening to UK Radio, playing British music twenty-four hours a day. Jangling guitar chimes introduced a song from The Smiths. *This Handsome Man.* If only that was what she wanted as an assistant.

Another mug of tea sat on the table opposite Ms Ryder's. A thin wisp of steam waved upwards toward the beams of the high ceiling. The thought about being in a hotel went through his mind again. He wished he was female at that moment so she would employ him. He wanted to stay there.

She looked up, a faint glint coming into her eyes again. "Oh, don't you look pretty in the gown."

He felt himself blush, his face warm. He put a hand to the front of the gown, concerned his penis might pop out. It was semi-hard against the gown. Her comment had an effect he hadn't expected. She had seen him naked earlier, but being hard would be a greater humiliation.

He thought she noticed the slight bulge, her eyes settling for a moment on the region below his waist. He was thankful she chose to ignore the situation.

"Take a seat, Amy. Sorry, I suppose I should call you David now we've established you're a man."

The heat in his cheeks burnt with embarrassment and he wondered if she was teasing him. He sat down opposite her. She pulled off her reading glasses and placed them on top of her papers. She put the pencil down and stared at the pile of papers by her hand.

"This is my latest book, Amy, I mean David, sorry. First edit." She took a breath and looked up at him. "Do you like my work?"

He gulped. What should he say? He didn't read books. They were boring.

"I haven't read any of your books. Yet, Ms Ryder."

He thought the *yet* might disguise his general lack of reading. He didn't want to annoy her. She studied his face as if trying to read him.

"So what types of book do you like, Amy." Her face was stern. "Sorry. David. I'll have to get used to that."

He winced. "I'm not much of a reader, Ms Ryder."

He thought it best to be honest, he guessed she would appreciate that. She considered his reply for a moment, then seemed to shake it out of her mind.

"You can stay here for tonight while I think about what I'm going to do with you. It's not fair to send you back after all you've been through getting here. I know you're reliable as Anne vouched for you. Anyway, your clothes are nowhere near dry."

He hadn't expected that. At least he wouldn't now have to walk back to the village and catch a bus back to Newbury. Fiona Ryder was so much kinder than his previous boss.

Fiona spotted his confused expression. "I called Anne while you were in the shower."

David took a sip of the hot tea, tugged on the dressing gown, then put the mug back on the table. Fiona Ryder's eyes widened, a cheeky look on her face.

"I berated Anne about not being clear you were a male."

His forehead creased. He wasn't sure what *berated* meant; Fiona Ryder used posh words like her friend Anne Dufort. He assumed *berated* was something to do with criticism or being told off? He could never imagine Anne Dufort taking criticism or being told off.

Fiona continued, "Anne told me you were gentle, reliable and sensitive." One of her eyebrows raised. "She told me you were quite girly, it's what she liked about you."

He tensed. "Ms Ryder, I can assure you, I'm a male."

She looked me over. "So I saw. Sort of."

He tensed again, a frisson of something sparked in his stomach. *Sort of?*

"I can see what Anne meant about you. With your long hair and female cut, slim body."

His face hardened.

"It's a compliment, David. Anne assured me you were perfect for me. I thought if you were indeed quite feminine, you *might* be what I need as an assistant. Who knows? Maybe you'd work out after all. But I need to think about it. I will speak with Anne again tonight."

This was beyond anything he could have hoped for. He put a hand to his chest as the anticipation rose. He wasn't sure what she was proposing. It seemed promising though.

"What do you mean, Ms Ryder?"

She placed both her slim elegant hands on the table as if she were playing a piano. Her manicured nails were a light shade of glossy blue with white ends.

"What I mean is you can stay one night. Tomorrow morning we can talk about it."

His heart jumped, pleased he might have a chance to prove to her he could do a good job for her. He knew this might be no more than a stay of execution. If she didn't want him, he'd be going back to London tomorrow and nothing will have changed. At least he could spend the night here, in the warm and with food. He would face the problems tomorrow.

"Thank you, Ms Ryder, I won't let you down if you give me this chance."

She sat back, withdrawing her hands. "Let's not get ahead of ourselves, David." I said I need to think about it and talk to Anne again. Let's see what tomorrow brings."

The music from the radio faded out and an announcer said it was 6 pm. A newsreader said they were going to the news headlines *at the top of the hour.* She began to speak. "The Prime Minister has announced a nationwide lockdown starting from tomorrow morning, 9 o'clock. They have reversed their earlier policy of no restrictions in an attempt to fight against the COVID-19 coronavirus."

Fiona listened a moment then turned back to David. "I wonder what that will entail?"

He had no idea what *entail* meant. He was about to find out.

Chapter 8 — A Change of Clothing

Fiona was lost in thought for a moment at the news announcement. She returned to the present predicament of finding David some clothing.

"David, I hung all your clothes on the line in the utility room. They are going to take all night to get dry. To be completely honest, I think your suit is ruined. As are your shoes. I think your underpants were at the end of their life anyway. Yuk."

David considered this for a moment. He would have to remain in the short dressing gown for the evening. Not ideal, but better than the alternative.

"I suggest you go up to your bedroom and I'll find you something else to put on."

He didn't understand what she would find.

"You can't go around in a short dressing gown all evening."

That much was true, he thought, it wasn't suitable. Potentially revealing and his legs were chilly. It wasn't as warm in the kitchen as in the bedroom upstairs. He wanted to put on socks, trousers and a jumper, some proper male clothes. To cover up.

"You have male clothing here?" he asked, surprised a female-only household might have a store of male clothes. Even more surprising if they fitted him.

"I have loads of clothing. I'll find something for you to put on."

He fidgeted. "I can't wear your clothing, Ms Ryder."

She looked surprised. "Nonsense, I have loads of clothes I no longer use." Her eyes sparkled with mischief. "You didn't have any problem coming here dressed in a woman's business suit."

He was shocked. "A woman's suit?"

She looked at him as if he were simple. "Yes, a woman's suit."

He shook his head. Anne Dufort had put him in female clothing? "I, I, I didn't know."

She snorted a gave a single shake of her head. "Don't tell me you didn't notice the jacket had a fitted waist and the trousers were shorter than normal with a side zipper. You can't be that naive."

His mouth dropped open. Anne Dufort had duped him? He looked down at the floor under the table. "I didn't know." Anger built inside him at what Anne Dufort had done to him. She had put him in female clothes for two years. No wonder people had referred to him as a Miss.

Fiona nodded to herself. "Anne did say you weren't going to win the Brain of Britain Award anytime soon."

He ignored her put down. He felt stupid enough. So that was why the suit was so tight and short. He thought it was the latest style. Lots of young men wore styles like this these days. He had wondered about the side zip on the trousers, now he knew. He wouldn't fall for that again.

"I'll find you something suitable. Trousers, blouse, footwear. They won't be any more feminine than what you've been wearing."

They would certainly be better than the gown he had on, he thought.

"Go and wait in your bedroom and I'll bring up some clothes for you to wear tonight. It looks like we're a similar size, maybe I'm a little bigger." She tapped her pencil on the table.

David got up reluctantly. He knew he had to be grateful to her and he had to try to impress her if he was to stand a chance of getting this job.

"Thank you so much, Ms Ryder. I won't let you down."

"Good boy," she said. "Now get yourself upstairs and I'll bring those clothes in for you."

* * *

Thirty minutes later, David rummaged through the clothing Fiona had placed on the bed in a neat, folded pile. There was a pair of black trousers, a white blouse and a plain yellow tee shirt. These were not so bad, however, there was also a packet of panties, still wrapped in cellophane, and a pair of tights which was also labelled pantihose. They were packed in a cardboard cover with a cellophane window. He ran his fingers through his hair. The tights were fine nylon, shiny and black.

Fiona had left a pair of black shoes on the floor by the bed. They were plain but had a single strap over the top and a wide heel about two inches high. A heel? They wouldn't be easy to walk in. At least the heels were wide. Anne Dufort had never asked him to wear heels. He saw the writing along the edge of the inner liners: Mary Jane. He assumed this was the name of the manufacturer. They would have to do, it was only for one night. A thought came to him that would have to wear them to travel back home to London if Fiona decided she wanted to keep looking for a female assistant. This was a big probability.

He slipped off the dressing gown and picked up the plain white blouse. It wasn't too different to what he had been wearing for Anne Dufort. David held it up on the hanger and ran his fingers down the fine cotton material. The blouse was shaped at the waist, a little more than the ones he had been wearing before. He put it on and buttoned it up. It was a good fit although loose in the chest area.

He ripped open the pack of panties. There were five sets in white, powder blue, yellow, pink and a light purple. The cotton was thin, soft and there was a tiny bow on the front of each one. These were going to have to do. Maybe these female panties weren't so different to male underpants, a bit thinner and smaller, but they would do. If he wore the white ones or the blue ones then it would be fine. It was just for one night.

He wiped a bead of sweat from his forehead, was it the heat or was it that his legs wobbled at the thought of this clothing? He pulled the panties on. They felt good, snug and his penis and testicles were outlined inside the light material. He stomach turned as if there was a feather floating inside. Growth started in his penis at the sensation. He felt light-headed.

There were no socks, his only option was to wear the pantyhose tights, otherwise his feet would rub inside the shoes. He pulled them up over his feet and lost balance and fell on the bed. This was harder than he expected. He tugged them up to his waist. His leg hairs were plastered to his leg like thousands of dark veins.

He pulled on the black trousers she had provided. He wanted to look good for Fiona, anything that helped to make her consider him for the role would be useful. The zipper was on the side, like his suit trousers. He felt himself redden as he remembered this was the style for girls and he had been wearing female trousers for two years to work. He shrugged and tucked in the blouse. It looked better that way, it hid the taper. Everything fitted perfectly. They were nice quality, nothing he could have afforded. But. They were girls' clothes. This time he knew it.

He picked up the plain black shoes. The wide heel would be fine, it would give him a bit of height. He needed that.

It was time to return downstairs. He went to the shower room and brushed his hair. He tried to push it to one side, to make it less female looking. It was clean and bouncy, a little fizzy after the rain. It would have to do. He inspected himself in the mirror. Everything looked more fitted than his usual clothing, but it was plain enough. If no one knew they were female clothing, he might get away with it. The trousers were shorter than he would have liked; his ankles showed, wrapped in the fine nylon.

He stood straight and breathed deeply. "Here goes," he said to himself softly.

He went back downstairs and to the kitchen. The radio was on, playing light rock in the background. Fiona was chatting with a lady with a dark bob cut. It was the person he had seen in the back garden from the bedroom window. He hadn't expected anyone else to be there. He suddenly felt conscious of his femininity. Long blond hair and heels. Fiona and the other lady turned to look at him. The lady looked him up and down. A sneer crept over her face. She didn't seem friendly.

Chapter 9 — Enemy Contact

The lady was dressed in a dark-green jacket, tight black trousers and green rubber Wellington-style boots. She looked around the same age as Fiona, but more rounded and solid. Strong. Her bottom filled out the seat of her thick black leggings like two large firm melons.

The two women both stopped talking at the same time as they looked at him. He felt his face flush red in the sudden silence and embarrassment that he was standing in female clothes.

"David Amey, this is Ellen."Fiona looked back to the lady. "Ellen, David."

He walked towards them, holding out a hand to shake Ellen's. "Hello Ellen," he said.

Ellen raised both eyebrows and looked him and down as if assessing a rat. Her eyes alighted on his hair. "My, my, aren't you the pretty one." Her hands stayed by her side.

He stopped dead in his tracks, his handshake frozen in thin air. "What?"

Ellen pursed her lips. "I meant you look nicer than I had expected you might." She batted her eyes. "Considering you're dressed in girl's clothing and have a girl's hairstyle. You're very pretty."

"Wha...wha...what?" He stammered, not expecting to receive comments so direct.

Fiona dug Ellen in the ribs. "Stop teasing him." She turned back to him. "Your clothes look great, David, they're not *that* girly. Ellen's teasing you. She knows I had given you some of my clothes to put on. It's her little joke."

He wasn't convinced as Ellen's cold stare pierced into him. He could see the two women were very comfortable together.

Ellen sniggered. "What little joke, Fiona?"

Fiona poked her again. "You're terrible, Ellen."

Fiona continued to laugh as she walked away to the end of the kitchen to retrieve her book manuscript.

Ellen stared at him, coldness in her eyes. "Yes, it was a joke." Her eyes narrowed. "Amy," she whispered, out of range of Fiona's hearing.

Fiona returned. "David's staying the night. I'm going to decide whether to keep him on or not as my personal assistant."

Ellen nodded slowly, digesting and seeming to chew on Fiona's words. In the background, the radio had gone to a newsflash. The newsreader reminded the listeners the lockdown would start tomorrow at 9 am. The newsreader reminded everyone that no one was to leave their homes unless necessary, then went on to describe the rising number of victims of the virus.

David had a sudden thought. "I need to get back to London tomorrow to get my belongings."

"Don't worry, David. I'm sure it will be fine." I'll see you tomorrow in my office at the front of the house. We can discuss all this then. In the meantime please sit down. Ellen has prepared some food for dinner. Then we can all get an early night. I have a busy day tomorrow completing the draft manuscript and you've had a difficult day. With the journey and the weather."

He sat down at the kitchen table and laid his hands on the table. "But what if I can't get back to my apartment because of the lockdown?"

The two ladies weren't listening, they were getting the food ready and placing it on the table. He didn't feel relaxed about the new lockdown situation.

Chapter 10 — House Rules

David fidgeted in the chair by the side of Fiona Ryder's desk. A low morning sun filtered in through the window. He had an index finger in his mouth as he bit ferociously on a fingernail. He had started biting them again this morning without Anne Dufort's oversight. His clear nail varnish was chipping away with the attention of his gnawing teeth.

The low morning sun peered through the large picture window beside her desk. There was an eerie silence, only the occasional bird chirping from a large oak on the boundary of the front garden. Ms Ryder had opened a smaller window and the fresh scent of blossom floated in on the gentle breeze.

Fiona had told him to wait there for a few minutes, after telling him the virus events had taken a turn for the worse this morning.

On Fiona's desk lay a three-inch stack of paper, stacked neatly. He leant over to read the top page.

AN UNUSUAL MURDER

F L Ryder

Draft 1

Fiona Ryder, F L Ryder, the world-famous author and part-recluse. He remembered seeing her on the TV once or twice. He had looked her up again on the internet last night and read she was famous for her successful detective novels.

Her books were a series of stories about a maverick female police inspector, based in the English countryside. They had recently been made into a popular TV series. There was also talk of a film.

F L Ryder was renowned for being wealthy, beautiful, single and rarely gave interviews or TV appearances. She was also well known for being very demanding with her employees. He considered this was probably PR; she had been friendly and kind with him. Unlike Ellen.

He gazed around the room, holding his hands between his knees which he jiggled with impatience. The walls were an unmarked matt pale blue emulsion. Brilliant white skirting boards lined the bottom of the wall. A single large green-leafed shrub sat in a black pot in one corner. The entire wall behind him was filled with a white bookshelf full of books. He noticed each book was arranged alphabetically by author. He had never seen so many books in a home before.

His attention fell on a row of books by the same author as the young woman who had been reading on the train yesterday: *Lady Alexa*. He had never heard of this aristocratic author before and now she was everywhere. He would have to look this Lady Alexa person up on the internet later.

His face stung from the wet shave in the morning. He had found a pink disposable female razor in the shower room. It had been blunt and there was no shaving foam. Fiona expected him to be tidy and facial whiskers would not be a good look on his first day. He'd had to use shower gel as a lubricant. In combination with the blunt razor, it hadn't been perfect for the job. He had tried to look good for Ms Ryder, even if his face was a little scratched. He had learnt from Anne Dufort what strong women wanted.

He was wearing the black female trousers she had loaned him and the yellow tee-shirt. His legs were crossed, the top leg tight against the lower, calf against calf, as Anne Dufort had shown him. His tee-shirt was shaped with a low neckline. It was feminine and he was concerned about what might happen if he wasn't able to get some male clothes. He could ask Fiona to do a mail-order for him, the parcel delivery services should still be working.

He had been waiting more than ten minutes so far and he was getting bored. He tapped his Mary Jane shoes on the floor with irritation. It wasn't as if there was a TV to watch here, there was nothing to entertain him, just rows of neatly arranged books. At that moment Ms Ryder rushed in and sat down. She picked up the large pile of printed paper and tipped it on end and banged them on the table to put them in order. They already seemed perfectly arranged. A scent of sweet perfume trailed in behind her in her wake. She noted his neat leg cross.

"Right. David. This is what I've decided, although events have played a part in my final decision."

David put his hands between his knees. He was surprised to be nervous at what she might say. He screwed his eyes up, hoping.

"To start with, you're stuck here. You can't leave. The national lockdown is now in effect. So, since you're here, I'm going to employ you on a trial basis. For the next couple of weeks, you'll be working for me, as my assistant. Then we'll review things, once the lockdown eases and I can assess your performance myself. I know Anne thought you would be perfect for me, and I trust her, but I would like to see for myself."

David had been holding his breath. He let it out slowly. Relief flowed through him.

"Let me be clear," she continued, still fiddling with her manuscript papers. "Your job for these next couple of weeks, or so, will be to allow me to have a singular focus on my writing. I have a deadline to complete my draft. Your work here will be about ensuring I'm not distracted from this single focus. The new book. Is this clear, Amy? I mean David."

Her tone was soft and gentle with the underlying steeliness he had heard yesterday. He wanted to jump up and do a jig and then hug her. He had a job again, albeit temporary, and he had somewhere to live and food to eat. Then his excitement stopped. He was stuck there, how would he get back to his apartment to get his clothes? He didn't have time to ask Ms Ryder.

"Listen carefully," she said. "I have some house rules. I do not want to have to repeat them."

He nodded solemnly. "Yes, I understand, Ms Ryder." He put on his concentrated look, or what he thought it should look like.

"Firstly, The food is delivered from the supermarket once a week on Fridays, 11 am. Ellen orders it online. She'll order additional food for you and you'll eat what we eat, I'm not getting anything special in for you. But meals are part of your package. For your trial. I believe in healthy food, it's important for writers to remain healthy, all that sitting around isn't good for your health."

She looked up at the ceiling to think. He thought sitting around was fine.

"Point two. You'll shave every day and your hair will be brushed and styled. I don't like laziness or casual clothing on my employees. I do not like facial whiskers, especially as I thought you were going to be a girl." She framed her hands around her manuscript. "I insist on my employees looking good. Even Ellen, my gardener stroke cook stroke maintenance person stroke whatever is necessary, always looks good. I'm sure you noticed last night she was tidy and clean, even after a day working outside."

He creased his face up at the thought of Ellen. She had been decidedly unfriendly last night. She might be a problem. Something was not right with her attitude towards him.

Fiona Ryder continued. "Ellen's worked for me for years. She lives in a cottage on the other side of the field behind my house. She crosses the field to come here every weekday to cook dinner, look after my large garden and do various odd jobs and maintenance work around the home. I like her. She's no-nonsense and to the point.

Sometimes she brings her niece, Jenny, who lives with her. Jenny's a young girl, eighteen or so. Ellen put her forward for the job you'll be doing, but she was far too young and a bit childish. I need someone with experience and a little more maturity." She pointed at me. "Like you, I hope. Ellen was a little disappointed I didn't take her niece on but never mind. She'll get over it."

Ms Ryder put her papers down on the desk by her keyboard. She straightened the keyboard so it was in line with the edge of the desk and the manuscript papers. She moved her mouse so it was central.

David liked rules, they gave him structure. It gave him a guide, as Anne Dufort had done, despite her putting him in female clothing and getting his hair and nails done. None of Fiona's rules would be a problem.

"I've lost count of what rule we're on," she said, rubbing her chin with a thumb and forefinger. "Anyway. The next rule is breakfast in my study at 8. Lunch is at 12.30. You'll prepare them. Ellen, and sometimes Jenny, cook dinner for 8 pm. They cook, you will serve it. In between these times, you'll clean and tidy the house and bring me coffee and tea during the day. Maybe a snack of fruit, if I ask for some, or any other task I demand. Right?"

This all seemed simple. He liked simple. Follow her orders, no need to think too much. He nodded assent.

"This takes me to my final rule, clothing and hygiene. Anne bought you clothing for work and I also expect you to be well dressed every single day. At all times. And to be clean and tidy, hair, nails, everything. I don't get lots of visitors, but the ones I do are important people: publishers, my agent, journalists and marketing people. I know we're locked down right now, so we're going to have to make do somehow with whatever clothing I can find for you."

He rubbed his palms down his cheeks. *We're going to have to make do with whatever clothing I can find for you?* This wasn't working out after all. She hadn't finished.

"We will need to sort your fingernails out. I believe Anne took you to a hair salon and a nail salon?"

He nodded and turned his fingers over to hide them in shame. Now he had started biting them again, a couple were chipped and showing signs of his chewing.

"We can't take you to a nail salon to get you tidied up because of this damned lockdown and virus crisis. But Ellen has kindly offered that her niece, Jenny, will do your nails for you. She has some skill in this area, more than being a personal assistant, that's for sure. I've asked her to start on this today."

He didn't think this idea was attractive at all, Ellen was not exactly his best friend and he was sure that Jenny wouldn't be friendly either. He had the job she wanted. There had to be an ulterior motive here that he wasn't seeing. Why would Ellen offer to help?

Whatever Ellen's motives, he had to show willingness if he was to keep this job. He supposed that a little nail care was a small price to pay. The biggest embarrassment had been spending time in the nail salon as the only man. The clear nail varnish and slightly long nails were subtle enough. He needed to keep an eye on what Ellen was up to all the same.

As Ms Ryder considered her next point, he saw the opportunity to make a suggestion about his clothes.

"Ms Ryder, I have an idea about what to wear, since you want me to always be well dressed."

She raised her eyebrows. He took this as assent to carry on.

"You could order me a set of clothing online, to tide me over until this lockdown is finished. That way I can have male clothing and not wear your cast-offs."

Fiona shuffled on her seat. "I could, but I have far too much to do. I'm on a deadline for the release of my latest novel. It's at the editing stage and I don't have time to go looking for clothing for you online. Besides, you might only be here for a short so why would I go to the expense of buying you a full set of clothes when I have more than enough to pass on to you?"

"I'll sort it out," he offered.

"OK, if you have a credit card and money then go ahead."

He looked at the floor, he didn't. He had hoped she would do it for him, as Anne Dufort had done. He hadn't expected she would push back on him. His credit card had been blocked through non-payment of the bills and he had an overdraft of £465 in his bank which had blocked any transfers.

"I don't have any money, Ms Ryder"

"And I don't have the time or inclination, David."

Another idea came to him. "If you give me your credit card, I'll do it for you."

Her expression told him he had gone too far. "You most certainly cannot have my credit card, I'm not about to pass out my personal email and credit card details to anyone. Apart from Ellen, who I know and trust. No. I gave you a pair of trousers and the tops yesterday, they will be fine. Absolutely. There's no problem I can see with this arrangement for now. I will find you more unisex things to wear."

She seemed to be warming to her idea as he froze in horror at the implication of what she was saying. He didn't know what to say or do. She seemed set on the idea of him using her clothes.

"Yes, it'll be absolutely fine," she continued, warming to the idea even further. "I'm not sure I have any more spare trousers, but I'll see what I can find. Anyway, it's only us and Ellen here, I don't know what the problem is, even a skirt would be fine. It's just clothing."

His heart missed a beat, then thumped. She couldn't be serious. That was a joke. Wasn't it?

Chapter 11 — A Skirt is No Joke

The promise of a bright sunny day was fading behind darkening skies, as it so often did on early spring mornings. He studied Ms Ryder's face. Was she serious? *A skirt? Yes,* he thought, *it had to be a joke.*

He had to say something, in case she meant it. "I can't wear a skirt, Ms Ryder. Girls wear skirts and I'm a man."

She waved his comment away with a flick of a hand. "I have no idea why this social rule exists, if you think logically, it's an invention of society. Didn't men wear wigs and makeup in Elizabethan times? And frilly blouses? Anyway, you have a pair of trousers and they should suffice for now. You're on a trial so I don't want to go buying a new set of clothes only to decide you're not up to the job?"

His mouth went dry. She had a point there. "No, Ms Ryder, I suppose not. Anyway, I guess my clothes from yesterday are dry now so I can wear them."

"They were all ruined by the rain. Ellen told me this morning, I forgot to mention it. She threw them away. You'll have to wear what I find for you."

His jaw dropped. He had only one pair of trousers to last the lockdown period. How long would that go on?

She pushed her silvery hair away from her face. He guessed she dyed it at her age, but it looked perfect. Everything about her was perfect and stylish. Today she was in a loose white dress with small polka dots; she could have been at a cocktail party. Her legs were slim and bare. She seemed to be thinking about something, then sat up straight.

"You know I didn't want a male assistant. I much prefer employing females. Men can be such a pain to work with, all that macho stuff, your comments seem to show you're no different. Men can't seem to help themselves. And the explanations, mansplaining I've heard it called". She sounded a short 'mmmm' as she pondered him without blinking.

She looked over him as if she were a lioness surveying her prey.

"At least you're not all big and masculine looking." She looked me over again. "Yes, you are more than a little feminine looking, if I might say. I like that." Her eyes hovered over his hair. "But you'll wear what I say and do what I ask otherwise this is going to be a short trial."

She spoke softly, even though the message was tough. He knew not to react to what she had said and he supposed she didn't mean she would put him in a skirt. It was more important at this moment to try to keep on her good side, rather than argue about being called feminine.

"I'll do whatever you tell me, Ms Ryder. I have no complaints. Sorry."

She relaxed. "Good. I've already told you how much I hate any disruption to my writing," she said. "My writing is everything. Your job will be to do whatever I need and whatever I ask. You have to do everything without question so I can concentrate on writing. There is no 9 till 5, you'd be on duty 24/7. Focussed entirely on my needs."

That didn't sound so bad, being told what to do. "Yes, Ms Ryder," I said. "It won't be a problem."

"Good boy," she purred. She pursed her lips. However, it was clear she wasn't fully convinced. "I wanted a female." She sighed long and hard. "Men can be such bores. I hope you're not going to be a bore" She trailed off and seemed to be talking to herself. "The trouble is I haven't found anyone who wants to live here in the middle of the countryside and I'm having to do everything myself." She thought for a moment. "This is the offer, David. You'll have a private room and bathroom up in the converted attic for the period of your trial. I will provide all your food. You won't get any salary, but if your trial works out, we can discuss a small salary. I think it's a good offer considering you'll have no rent, energy or food costs."

There was no option. He would show her how good he was. "Thank you, Ms Ryder, that would be great." He tried to stifle his disappointment at a lack of wage with a watery smile.

His mind raced over how much rent and food money he would save. £1,200 a month in rent for starters plus around £500 a month for food and more for energy costs. Her no salary offer was worth around £2,000 a month. Plus, the idea of cutting and running from his debts raced through his mind. This might work out, after all. Lady Luck was back.

"I won't let you down," he said feeling better about the trial.

"Let's hope not," she grumbled. "There are a few rough edges I don't like about you, but they can be ironed out. I also reserve the right to admonish or even punish you for any errors you might make. I expect perfection in everything. I'm a successful author and I have no time for distractions caused by others, especially my hired assistant. Your job would be to serve me and be otherwise unobtrusive."

David didn't know what *unobtrusive* meant. He also didn't like where he thought this was going.

She continued. "You will need to learn to associate misbehaviour and errors with punishment. This will be an element of your training period, as I look to improve your spoken voice and diction. Your speech is harsh, it grates on me. I'm a writer, I like perfect grammar. And I also expect deference," she said, looking at him hard.

There it was again. Her long words. His mind turned over the word, *deference*. How was he supposed to follow her orders if she spoke using strange words?

"Part of your trial period will be to see if I can train you. Ellen's off work today, something to do with her niece feeling under the weather. Anyway, I'll ask her to help me, she knows what I like."

He hadn't heard the phrase *under the weather* since he was a child. "I think I can do what you say, I wouldn't want to bother Ellen though…," he said, hoping he could have as little contact with her as possible.

Fiona put a hand up. "It's no bother for her, she's always helped me. She's like the sister I never had, even though technically she's an employee. She'll be only too glad to help me get you to how I want you."

"I'm sure she would," he mumbled to himself.

She heard him. "That's the spirit," she replied cheerfully, missing his sarcasm or maybe ignoring it deliberately.

She put a finger under her chin. "Now, where was I? Oh yes. Also your comportment and deportment are not good. You slouch and shuffle, your manners are a bit rough. Let's see if we can tidy that up too. I want you to be more gentle, more refined. It will all be part of your trial. Ellen will be great at helping you."

He turned the words over in his mind. *Comportment, deportment.* What on earth did they mean? *Comport, compo...?*

Fiona saw his confused face. "It means your manners, conduct, behaviour and how you hold yourself; physically."

Why didn't she say that, he thought? *Instead of using words no one understood?*

Fiona turned back to her desk. "Don't fret though, Ellen will help you."

He didn't like the sound of this.

"You can go now. I think you can start with doing my washing and then the ironing. There's a pile in the utility room behind the kitchen."

She ushered him away with a wave of her hand. The interview was over. The hard work was to begin now. The hardest part being how to handle Ellen.

Chapter 12 — Housework Time

David left the office feeling light-headed. He told himself a little training wouldn't hurt. It was all part of the job, wasn't it? It had been good to have direction from Anne Dufort, so this would be good too. The snag was, Fiona Ryder was handing training over to Ellen.

David went first to the utility room to put the washing on. He stuffed the pile of dirty clothes laying on top of the work-surface into the washing machine There was also a pile of creased washed clothes in a large wicker basket. He found the ironing board, set it up and began his ironing work, humming under his breath. He enjoyed ironing, he didn't understand why people moaned about it. There was no need to think, you just did it.

All was quiet in the house and as Ellen was not working, this made it even better for him. He pottered around doing Fiona's chores for the rest of the day. It was a light day. He made coffees and teas for Fiona when she called him, and she remained working in her office. He thought this might work out, certainly for him.

Ellen had left a prepared meal of salad and cold meat for the evening which David brought to Fiona. She ate in her office, still working on the draft. He ate alone in the kitchen and took the opportunity for an early night. He knew this type of easy day was going to end. That would probably happen tomorrow, once Ellen returned.

Chapter 13 — A Pretty Sissy

The next morning, while he was pottering around the house cleaning, Fiona called David into her office. She explained she had a bell in the office and she would ring it if she needed something. He didn't like the idea but what could he do?

In the mid-afternoon, the first tinkle of the bell sounded. He switched off the vacuum cleaner, hurried from the living room where he had been working, and to her office and burst in. She looked startled, then her face dropped into a stern look he hadn't seen before.

"David. You need to knock first, even when I've called you. This is my workplace and I may be in the middle of something."

He stuttered an apology. Ms Ryder was different to his previous employer, but every so often he saw a touch of steel behind her kind exterior.

"Not to worry, I know this is all new for you. I'm sure you'll pick it up." Her face softened again and the atmosphere thawed. "Would you be a sweetie and bring me a coffee. I need a shot of caffeine to liven me up during this editing."

He left and walked into the kitchen. Ellen was leaning against the kitchen work-surface, munching on a biscuit. A pair of lightly soiled garden gloves lay on the table. She smiled a fleeting rictus grin and popped the remains of the biscuit into her mouth. She chewed slowly, all the time looking at him behind a thin sneer.

She swallowed. "Well if it's not pretty little Amy." She searched in the packet for another biscuit.

"My name's David."

"If you say so. You look more like an Amy to me. Especially in those girly clothes and with the pretty hairstyle."

His lip curled. "I'll tell Fiona what you're saying."

He instantly regretted saying that. Ellen sniggered. He knew Fiona was fond of Ellen, it wouldn't do to make a scene. He walked past her. He needed to get to a cupboard behind her.

"Excuse me, Ellen, I need to get to the coffee jar. Fiona's asked for coffee."

Ellen moved slowly to one side to allow space. He reached into the cupboard to get the coffee and then put water into the kettle to boil. Ellen's eyes burnt into him.

"I bet you can't wait to get into a pretty dress. You only have one pair of trousers, so it's a matter of time. You can't wear them every day. I'm looking forward to that moment too. I'm sure Fiona wants it too, although she doesn't know it yet. She wants an all-female working environment." Ellen considered her words as she stroked her chin. "I suppose she has one in reality. You being a pretty sissy."

He ignored her jibes. He was sure she would eventually get bored with it. Her comment about him having just one pair of trousers concerned him though. That was a painfully correct fact. What was he going to do when they needed washing? And his hair. He resolved to ask Fiona to trim it for him. Short. This would stop one line of attack from Ellen.

Ellen wasn't yet bored. "It would be better if you were in a skirt. The sooner the better. Girls should wear skirts and you are very girly." She lifted a lock of his shoulder-length hair as if to prove the point.

He slammed down a mug. "Stop it," he snapped.

He had always had a temper, it didn't take much. She had pushed him to his limit.

Ellen didn't flinch. "I'll leave you to your girly housemaid duties. I have real work to do outside. See you for dinner."

She walked to the back door then stopped and turned. "See you later. Amy."

She opened the back door and a chilly breeze gusted in. The weather had turned cooler again. She closed the door behind her and the chill was cut off instantly.

He now knew this was going to be a lot tougher than he had expected. Ellen was clearly annoyed about her niece not getting his job and was determined to goad him into a reaction. He finished making Fiona's drink and returned to her office. He knocked and waited. He decided not to tell Fiona about what had just gone on.

"Come in." Her voice was muffled from behind the closed door.

He entered and walked up to her, placing the hot mug on her desk. Her window was closed. Outside the sun was a low murky disc shining weakly from behind low clouds.

"David," she said. "I'd like you to acknowledge me when you do something. So I know you've understood and will act on what I've asked for. You're not very demonstrative, are you?

There she goes again, long words. Was she even speaking English? Why couldn't she use normal short words? How's anyone supposed to know what she's on about?

"A small bow of the head or drop of the knee is fine, nothing too ostentatious."

His face creased and frowned. What the hell did *ostentashalous* mean, or whatever it was she had said? He nodded his head down as she had asked all the same.

"Thank you, dearie. I suggest you can take the rest of the day off and relax in your room.

Come down for dinner at 7 pm. We'll all eat together in the kitchen tonight. Won't that be nice? A chance for you and Ellen to get to know each other better." She dismissed me with an absent-minded flick of her hand.

He waited, summoning up the courage to ask her to cut his hair for him. Here goes, he thought. "Ms Ryder, please, I need to ask you a big favour."

She stopped typing. "What?" She snapped, then recommenced her typing.

"Would you mind cutting my hair? I think it's too long. Too feminine."

"Get out."

He scurried out the door. He was going to be stuck with the long hair. At least he was grateful for some rest and to have the chance for a short sleep. It had been a strange day. Surely it could get any stranger?

Chapter 14 — Babydolls and Panties

Fiona seemed not to notice the chill between David and Ellen at dinner in the evening. David tried to be on better terms with Ellen; she was not interested.

He cleared up after they had eaten and stacked the dishwasher while the two ladies chatted over a drink. Despite the afternoon nap, he felt weary again.

Fiona spotted this. "Right, my dear. You can go to bed now as you need to be up for 7 am. Ellen reminded me you don't have any nightwear. The nights can get chilly so Ellen has sorted out something for you to wear. She brought it over for you from her home, she has never worn it so I'm sure it will be fine."

Outside the wind was whipping up and the sound of rain splattering on the patio stones by the back door infiltrated the kitchen space. Fiona slid her chair away, scraping it on the tiled floor with a shrill screech. She went to the next room and returned with something red, wrapped inside a cellophane packet. Ellen watched intently.

"Isn't this nice of Ellen, she's so thoughtful." Fiona touched Ellen affectionately on her forearm.

David took the packet and muttered. "Thank you." His tone was flat as he didn't think this looked good. Whatever was in the packet was a red satin material. He could see a lace trim.

Ellen watched with studied interest. "I think he should try it on for us, Fiona. To make sure it fits."

He looked at both of them in horror.

Fiona clapped her hands once. "Yes, it's a good idea, Ellen." She turned to him. Go next door and change into it and come back to show us."

He nearly dropped the packet. *She can't be serious*, he thought? He saw she was deadly serious. He opened the bag and placed the cellophane on the table. He shook out the red clothing. The material felt like satin, but he guessed it was a synthetic substitute. He held it up by the two thin shoulder straps. "It's a baby-doll nightie," he whined. "This has to be a joke."

Fiona's expression told him it wasn't.

Ellen spoke, "Go and put it on, Amy."

David ground his jaw at Ellen's instructions. Fiona seemed not to notice her jibe, calling him Amy.

"Try it on, David," Fiona added. "If it's too small I can find you something else to wear." Fiona's voice was as gentle as ever, her instruction firm. "David. I want you to try it on. Now run along, put it on and come back so we can see if it fits. Ellen's kindly donated her own nightwear for you. It's the least you can do to show some gratitude. I don't want to have to ask you again."

He had to put it on. He slunk out and into the dining room next door, a pressure in his temples. Ellen was getting the better of him. He heard the two ladies chatting in the kitchen as he removed his clothing. He left his panties on as he slipped the red baby doll over his head and shoulders. It fitted like a glove against his slim body. He slumped in despair, he'd hoped it would not. He didn't believe for a moment this was Ellen's nightie, she was broader than him.

He smoothed it down, trying to get some length. His panties showed, the baby-doll was far too short to cover them. He rubbed both hands down the side of his body. The material was smooth and glossy. The lace around the hem was the same colour as the body of the nightie and flicked softly against his panties. The pressure now pounded in his temples and there was a movement in his penis. His body felt like jelly. There was a light gentle erotic feeling about the nightie.

"Hurry up, David. Does it fit? Come and show us."

Fiona's voice shot into the dining room, breaking him out of his trance. He took a deep breath and walked into the kitchen. The two ladies stopped talking. Fiona observed him for a moment.

"It looks fine. Good. You can use that."

Ellen glared, a look of contentment on her face. He was exposed and on some kind of show for the two women. He wanted to run, to curl up, to be invisible. Anything but to be there: humiliated, emasculated and embarrassed. His penis twitched and shot into an instant erection. Horror, this nightmare was getting worse by the second.

"I think she likes it," Ellen's voice was rich like flowing honey, dripping with satisfaction.

"Yes, it's excellent. Say thank you to Ellen," said Fiona.

Could this get any worse? He looked to the floor. "Thank you, Ellen." His penis burst to its maximum erection. He placed two hands over it. *Please let me escape,* he thought, *no more of this.*

"Good boy," Fiona said. "Now run along and get a good night's sleep. Good night." She seemed oblivious to his erection.

He rushed to the kitchen door.

"Ahem." It was Fiona. *What now?*

He spun around.

"Aren't we forgetting something?"

He stared back, not having a clue what she was on about.

"Dip a knee and say thank you."

For a short moment he didn't understand. Then he remembered the conversation in her office. A nod or dip of the knee to acknowledge her instructions. He didn't know what to do. He saw Ellen waiting with glee, her eyes dancing brightly. He was stuck in a vortex of intense humiliation.

A thought came to his mind. He could tell Fiona Ryder to stick her job where the sun doesn't shine. He didn't need to be humiliated like this. He hadn't minded when it was just the trousers and blouse and the two of them. But now there was a baby-doll nightie and Ellen had a slight smile across her lips again. What the hell, he needed to get this over with.

He closed his eyes and dipped a knee an inch and said. "Thank you, Ms Ryder." His face burnt with humiliation. He deliberately used Ms Ryder, ignoring Ellen. Small victories.

"Good boy. Now off you go, it will be a big day tomorrow. There is so much to do."

"Goodnight, Ms Ryder." He glared over at Ellen. "Ellen."

"Amy." Ellen's eyes sparkled.

He left the kitchen and ran up the stairs to his room went to his room and shut the door behind him. He threw himself on the bed, a lump in his throat and a raging erection below. The curtains blew wildly into the room. Someone had opened the windows earlier. Splashes of rain were coming in and dotting the floorboards. He pulled himself up and pulled the curtains and closed the windows. He put a hand on his erection, his panties were damp with pre-cum, the baby doll light around his waist, the thin shoulder straps fine and smooth. The lace around his chest tickled.

He pulled his erection out of his panties on impulse and rubbed it enthusiastically without thinking. He came into a cupped hand. His body shook in spasms as he ejaculated into his palm.

"Well, well. You like being a sissy girl."

He froze for a microsecond then turned around. Ellen was standing in the doorway, his clothes across her arm.

"Fiona asked me to bring these up for you, you'd left them downstairs. Her eyes were all over his limp, dripping penis and his hand, cupped full of his viscous cum. She screwed her face up. "Disgusting."

Outside the wind strengthened and whistled through the trees. The gushing sound of hundreds of leaves being whisked around the garden swished in from outside. Rain spattered hard against the windows.

Ellen dropped his clothes on the floor and left.

This had to be the worst moment of his life.

Chapter 15 — Trouble with a Capital E

"Wake up, wake up."

Inside his deep dream, he was being shaken.

"Wake up."

His eyes shot open. Someone was standing over him. He turned onto his back, angry at being disturbed. There was an unusual tightness across his shoulders, it was as if he had thin straps across them. A feeling of soft satin fluttered across his stomach.

A woman was standing over him, dark bobbed hair around her face, dressed in a green jacket and tight black trousers with knee-high boots. He rubbed his eyes with the balls of his hands.

She shook him again. "Get up girly. You are in big trouble. It's nearly a quarter past eight and Fiona was waiting for her breakfast. Luckily, my niece Jenny was here so she did it for her."

It was Ellen. He woke instantly. He shook his head once. Ellen's hands went to her hips. He rubbed his eyes again.

"I suggest you get up, get dressed, splash your face and go downstairs to apologise to Fiona. She is one unhappy lady."

Ellen's face was ruddy as if she had already been outside working in the cool morning air. She probably had. He sat up and went to pull the covers away then remembered he had the baby-doll nightdress on and whipped them back.

"Don't worry, I'm leaving. I don't want to see your little floppy clitty again." She walked to the bedroom door then turned back. "You're not going to last long as Fiona's assistant if you carry on like this. She hates laziness and being let down. Let's hope then." Ellen threw him a short hard stare and left.

David jumped out of bed feeling tension. His eyes flicked around the room. Should he shower? Should be get dressed and go straight to Ms Ryder and apologise. He went to move to the bathroom then stopped. He went to the wardrobe and grabbed the white blouse and trousers he had hung up there last night. Last night when Ellen had caught him masturbating. He remembered standing, a hand full of his cum. Her cold stare. His penis jerked again. *No surely not, not her?*

He squeezed his hands together, they were clammy. He needed to shower quickly. How could he have been so stupid? *Shit, shit, shit, shit.* His dream job and he might have thrown it away on the second day by oversleeping. What would Ms Ryder say to him? He went to the bathroom and showered inside two minutes. He dried himself and threw the towel on the floor. He returned to the bedroom and dressed in the blouse and dark trousers. He glanced at the clock on the bedside unit: 8.25. He went down the stairs with trepidation. What had he done? How could he have been so stupid?

His legs were weak and his face sweaty, despite the cool shower. He lurched down from the first floor to the next flight of stairs to the ground floor. He arrived at Fiona's office door. It was shut. He closed his eyes and stood a moment. The muffled clacking sound of keyboard keys being tapped at high speed was the only noise. He rapped on the door.

"Come in." Ms Ryder's voice sounded distracted as the clicks of the keyboard continued from behind the door.

He put his hand on the brass door-handle and twisted. He pushed the door open and shimmied in. She stopped typing and continued to look at the screen in front of her. There was a smell of lemon polish and fresh rain from the perpetually open window. A curtain waved from a gentle breeze.

Fiona was sitting at her writing desk, side on to him. The familiar pile of A4 paper was piled neatly by her right hand next to a slim silver keyboard. A printer was churning out paper to her side, the mechanical grinding sound repetitive.

She looked over to him and indicated he come to her with two wiggles of her index finger. He shuffled towards her, head bowed and hands clasped together across the front of his trousers. She had a way of making him feel small, like a schoolmistress to a schoolboy. In some strange way, he liked it. This was crazy, he knew that. She was beautiful, rich and famous. Maybe he was starstruck?

There was a different tension around her this morning. He knew he had distracted her from her work. He didn't want to look into her large brown eyes, he knew they would be drooping at her deep disappointment at his carelessness, his forgetfulness. At him distracting her from her work and her concentration.

"Look at me, Amey." She said, using his surname. This was not a good sign. She usually used David.

He shuddered with embarrassment every time she called him Amey. He had a first name, he was a thirty-five-year-old man.

He looked up. "Yes, Ms Ryder," he mumbled.

"I'm disappointed in you. This is a critical moment in my book and you've disrupted it. I said you should do nothing that resulted in any distraction from my work. My work is paramount. It's my life. I had to ask Ellen and Jenny to help as you were not here."

Her glare was unblinking, her hands on her knees. Her dark dress was splayed out from her small waist to her smooth knees. A gold pendant hung down between the deep crevice in her tanned breasts. Her hair was pulled back in a long ponytail this morning, giving her a sterner look.

"Yes, Ms Ryder, I'm sorry. It won't happen again, I forgot. I was tired."

She sniffed out through her nostrils like a frustrated horse. "These are all excuses and I'm not interested in them. Anne told me you were reliable, but it seems maybe you're not after all. I'm not sure what to do with you." She retreated into thought. "Ellen reminded me she has a niece who could replace you. Indeed, it was Jenny who stepped in this morning. She is certainly willing, if not entirely able."

David cringed. "What? You're going to replace me?"

"I didn't say that. I'm telling you what happened." She stared hard.

"Ms Ryder, I swear I won't let you down again. Please keep me on. I wasn't thinking straight. I'll put it right, I promise." He clasped his hands together, in an imitation of prayer.

Fiona puffed out her cheeks. "I don't know. Ellen's niece was the one here this morning to see to my breakfast, not you. She is female which is preferable. The trouble is she's only eighteen and not too mature. I don't know what to do."

He pleaded again. "I promise, I won't ever let you down again. Tell me what you want and I'll do it. Anything."

Fiona pondered, a slim finger against her cheek. "You will do anything I want? I wanted you to prepare breakfast this morning at 7.30."

David was desperate. "It won't happen again. Anything you tell me to do, I'll do. Anything."

"She considered this. "Anything?"

"Yes, if you keep me on?"

She thought about this. "If I do then there will be no more chances. You'll be punctual and do everything I ask. OK?"

He put a hand across his chest and a tentative smile creased across his face. She was wavering. He had a second chance. "Thank you, Ms Ryder." His smile broadened and his shoulders broadened. "What can I do for you? Say what you need."

She looked him up and down and her face darkened. "Well, I do like that attitude. Anything? "She chewed on the idea for a few moments. "The first thing you can do is something about your untidy look. You're wearing the same clothes as yesterday and the creases in your trousers are falling out. I don't like that. I told you there was a dress code; well-dressed and stylish. I can't abide scruffy clothing and today you look scruffy."

She ran a finger over his scuffed-up trousers.

"Go and iron them." She considered the again. "You wore them all day yesterday for work and they are dusty. Find something else to wear and put them on a quick wash." She turned back to her computer.

He nodded. Then remembered they were the only pair he had. "I don't have anything else to wear."

Fiona blew through her cheeks and froze. "Go and find something else." She spoke through gritted teeth. "I'm trying to work. If there is a second disruption then you will be out, lockdown or no lockdown." She didn't move for an instant, trying to bring her temper back under control. She resumed typing, hitting each key with more force than was necessary.

He took the cue and left. He had messed up. He wandered into the kitchen in a daze. Sitting at the table were Ellen and a young blond-haired girl. Each cupped a mug of coffee in their hands. They stopped talking when they saw him. He decided his best option this morning was to be friendly.

"Hello, you must be Jenny. Thank you for doing Ms Ryder's breakfast for me. I'm sorry I over-slept."

Jenny and Ellen swapped glances. "No problem," said Jenny, her young face had a hint of sarcasm.

"I assume you got a telling off," Ellen said. "Fiona likes order and structure. Everything has to be on time, regular and in its place. We got you out of a problem this morning, girlie."

He nodded, ignoring her jibe calling him a girlie. "Thank you, Ellen."

Ellen appeared more relaxed during the morning, despite her *girlie* comment. Maybe she had come round to accepting him in the household, he wondered. She had gone upstairs to wake him, so that was helpful. Maybe she could help with his problem with finding another pair of trousers? He explained Fiona wanted him to wash and iron his trousers as they were scruffy, but he had nothing else to put on.

He thought he saw a ghost of a smirk cross Ellen's lips. "I'm sure I can help you."

He didn't like the look on her face, had he made a mistake? Was he too trusting?

"Wait a moment." She said and left the kitchen.

He smiled at Jenny. She smiled back by screwing up her eyes only and said nothing. He waited for Ellen to return as a wall clock ticked. The sound of a tractor working in the fields beyond the back garden came into the kitchen.

"Thanks again," he said to break the silence.

She inclined her head to acknowledge him. Ellen returned. She handed him a black satin gown. "Put this on."

He took it and put it on. It was a mid-thigh Chinese-style gown.

"It's mine for when I stay over at Fiona's. It's all I could find. Now take your trousers off and Jenny will put them in the wash and then she'll hang them up, they should dry quickly in the wind outside."

He wrapped the gown around his waist and removed his trousers underneath.

"It's OK, I can wash and hang them up," he said

"Nonsense," said Ellen. "You need to get work done before Fiona gets angry with you again. Jenny will do this. Come back in a couple of hours and they will be clean and dry."

That made sense and it was a welcome change of approach from Ellen. From aggressive to helpful. Something in his mind told him not to trust her. But, she was right, he did need to get some work done. To make it up to Ms Ryder, to show her he was a responsible person. He handed his trousers to Jenny.

"Come back in two hours," Ellen said.

Was he making a mistake? What were they up to? They probably had a sticky start, there should be a feeling of comradeship amongst Fiona's employees. That was it. He walked back into the hall. The gown was soft and gentle. The Mary Jane shoes looked out of place, like two diver's boots on the end of his thin legs and a pretty gown. A pretty gown? It did feel nice. With the belt done up around his waist, it looked like a wrap-around dress. He closed his eyes and told himself not to be ridiculous.

He looked back towards the kitchen. Ellen and Jenny had their heads close together as if plotting. They were giggling. That could only mean bad news.

Chapter 16 — Shrinking Masculinity

He had his eyes on the clock. It was discomforting cleaning in what seemed like a dress and he was counting down the two hours until his trousers would be ready. He felt vulnerable. It was good of Jenny to wash and dry them for him, but he was apprehensive. Something didn't feel right and he didn't know exactly what. What could they do? No, he decided, all would be fine.

Ms Ryder rang her bell and called him for a coffee. He went to the kitchen and made it. Ellen and Jenny were nowhere to be seen. The washing machine was spinning in the utility room. He took in the coffee for Ms Ryder. She had given a disapproving look at his gown and mumbled he should think about dressing properly. She hadn't completely forgiven him yet. She returned to her typing, absorbed in her work. The sooner he could get back into trousers the better, he thought.

At midday, he wandered back into the kitchen. Ellen and Jenny were not there. He heard them whispering in the utility room and walked through and they were having a chat about something they were finding amusing.

"Hello, ladies, what's going on? Are my trousers done?"

They fell into giggles. He frowned, thinking they were being childish. They forced themselves to stop.

"Yes, they're done," Ellen said.

They both cracked up into peals of laughter. With a strong sense of being in the dark and a growing irritation at the two women, his eyes flitted around the room, searching for his clothing. The two women's giggles continued, increasing his sense of anger. He tugged his gown together and moved behind them.

"Was she really jerking off last night, Auntie? How gross."

He spun round in anger. Ellen was holding up his trousers.

"We had a *lickle* problem," Ellen said in a little girl's voice. They both dissolved into fits of laughter again, bending double.

He snatched the trousers from her and held them up. They were half the size they had been. He turned them over in his hands as if it were an illusion and they would revert to the correct size. They had shrunk, or they had been shrunk to be more accurate.

"We didn't notice the washing machine was set on maximum heat. They shrunk a little. It was an honest mistake," Ellen said. "Sorry," she added with no emotion.

"You did this on purpose," he snarled, wishing wasn't happening.

"Hello?" It was Ms Ryder's voice from the kitchen. "Where are you all? I need a break from my work."

David walked into the kitchen, to complain about Ellen and Jenny's latest trick. Fiona smiled, rubbed the back of her neck and stretched out. He hoped she had forgiven him. She was filling the kettle with water. She put it on and searched in the cupboards for the coffee. She brushed away a few strands of hair that had come adrift from her ponytail. Her eyes sagged.

"Why are you still in the gown? I thought I'd told you to put on something more suitable?" She was re-doing her ponytail, twisting the band around her fingers.

David held up the shrunken trousers. "Ellen shrunk them."

Ellen entered. "It was an accident, Fiona."

Ms Ryder looked as if she was about to scream. She took a moment and composed herself. "Go and find some proper clothing this moment. My patience is at an end. Amey."

David lowered the shrunken evidence of his trousers with mounting horror. She wasn't interested. "But, my only pair of trousers have shrunk. Ellen did it on purpose."

Fiona slammed a hand on the kitchen worksurface. "Stop whining, I can't abide whining." Her hand remained on the surface. "Ellen?"

Ellen pushed past him. "Yes, Fiona?"

"Get him out of my sight. Take him upstairs to his bedroom and then go and find something for him to put on from my personal wardrobe. Anything, sort him out for me." She turned back to David. "I don't want to see you moping around the house in a dressing gown or whining. Now. Go." She looked at the ceiling and spoke mainly to herself. "I don't know why I'm bothering with him." She gave a toss of her refitted pony tail as if to indicate the discussion was closed.

Ellen smirked at Ms Ryder's words then indicated to him he follow her, a small complacent smile remained etched across her face. He followed Ellen up the stairs and to his bedroom. Things were spiralling out of control and the unease was increasing with every step. He could not believe he had fallen into this situation. Had it been a trap set by Ellen or incompetence? Either way, she was finding his predicament highly amusing.

Ellen left him in his bedroom and he sat on the bed dejected. She returned within a couple of minutes. She was holding up a short flowing black skirt with pink dots and loose pleats. She removed it from the hanger and held it out to him. He pushed it away.

"It's either this or something even more girly. You choose." Ellen was in high spirits.

He snatched at the black skirt petulantly. It had a chiffon feel, fine and flowing. He didn't understand how he had got himself into this ridiculous situation. He was out of options. He felt weary, fed up with the struggle against Ellen. She had cornered him. Every time he thought he had got around her latest trick, she outwitted him. He stood, removed the gown, and let it fall to the floor. It was Ellen's and letting it drop was a small victory of sorts. Ellen's eyes fell to the small bulge in his panties. She smirked. A small surge in his penis was not the reaction he had expected or wanted. She noticed.

"I knew you'd like wearing a skirt, girly Amy. And don't even think about masturbating again.

Makes me feel sick at the thought of seeing you there jerking off last night."

He huffed and pulled the skirt up quickly to avoid her continuing gaze at his growing erection.

She was pleased. "It suits you, girly. Have you ever worn a skirt before, Amy? If not, why not?"

She circled him.

"Nice."

His anger fell away, he was defeated. The soft material around his legs had a calming effect. Ellen beckoned him. He followed her back down the stairs, the skirt soft and pleasant around his bare legs. There was a freedom and lightness he had never experienced in trousers. The air flowed around his legs and up to his erect penis. It was exciting and humiliating. And about to get worse as he entered the kitchen where Ms Ryder and Jenny were leaning against the units, coffee mugs in their hands.

Ms Ryder huffed. "That wasn't so difficult, was it. Thank you, Ellen, at least someone is keeping things in order."

He let his head drop and sat at the table to avoid being the centre of attention; standing in front of the three women in a pretty skirt was humiliating in the extreme. The skirt hung down from his thighs, his thin hairy knees protruded. This caught Ellen's attention.

"Fiona, would you like me to shave her legs, they look so ugly with all that hair."

Ms Ryder appeared to take no notice of Ellen's comment. He guessed she had heard perfectly well, but chose to ignore her. The back door was open beyond the utility room and a cold breeze circled in and around the kitchen. The hairs on his legs rose in the chill and he shuddered. Fiona did notice that.

"Ellen, why don't you find Amey a pair of warm tights, pantihose? He's cold with those bare legs. I bought a couple of pairs, they'll be in the left of my wardrobe. I'm surprised you didn't think of that. Why don't you pop back upstairs and find a pair for him."

Ms Ryder went over to David and rubbed his bare arm. It was an unexpected action.

"And it's a nice cardigan too. Ellen, you can be a bit thoughtless at times."

This was the first time he had heard Ms Ryder criticise Ellen, although it was mild. He saw

Ellen was disconcerted by the gentle rebuke and her face flushed and stiffened.

"Yes, Fiona." Ellen's hands went momentarily to her mouth.

He thought he may have seen her eyes water. She walked towards the door to the hallway and stopped. She flashed an aggressive, humourless smile at him. At that moment he realised there was little point in trying to please her. Ellen stomped out. She trampled up the stairs with heavier than usual footsteps. The kitchen fell into an uncomfortable silence. Jenny shuffled back into the utility room, mumbling about some leaves needing sweeping in the garden.

He was going to have to manage the situation if it wasn't to spiral further out of control. He had to fight back against Ellen. Not in an obvious way, but to find a way to nullify her attempts to antagonise and humiliate him. It was obvious, everything she had done was meant to humiliate him and to show Fiona her niece was a better option for his job. It was his job, he thought, and Jenny was not having it. He was not going to let her win. This was a dream job, despite the current clothing situation. He was sure that would be resolved once Ms Ryder had completed her manuscript and could find some time to buy him some male clothes. And when the lockdown has finished. It shouldn't be long.

In the meantime, he resolved to do everything Ms Ryder asked as he had promised, whatever it was and to make her life as easy as possible. That would blunt Ellen's plan. He was going to show Ellen up for what she was, he was going to be compliant and respectful in everything. She would have no reason to complain to Ms Ryder and, if she did, it would be her who look petty, not him. Yes, that would be his strategy. Even if it meant wearing a skirt. He could pretend he enjoyed it. It wasn't so difficult and it would blunt Ellen's strategy. He wasn't going to give up. This was war.

He noticed Ms Ryder watching him; she had spotted he was deep in thought.

"Don't worry about Ellen, she's not used to someone else in her little domain. She'll become accustomed to the situation in time, I shouldn't worry too much, Amy."

Amy? He asked himself why she had gone back to calling him by his last name?

"It's David, Ms Ryder. Amey is my surname."

She looked me over, analysing and assessing me. She nodded. "I know but Anne called you Amy and I think of you as Amy. In the circumstances, it now seems appropriate."

She looked him over again, sitting in the lightly pleated chiffon skirt and blouse. His long hair lay around his neck. Did she mean...?

Ms Ryder continued, "It's more appropriate calling you by your surname. You're my assistant and housekeeper. We should keep things formal."

He relaxed, he hadn't realised his body had tensed. He was expecting her to say a girl's name was more appropriate as he looked more like a girl. Yes, it was his surname and that had to be the explanation. She couldn't have meant anything else.

Chapter 17 — Clothes Make The Girl

Ms Ryder ran a hand over his arm once more, to soothe his frayed mood. Her rich perfume wafted around him, a whisper of a grin across her lips.

"I have to say, these clothes do suit you." She put a finger to her lips and stifled a giggle.

He melted at her attempt at kindness, while his face and neck burned with embarrassment at her words.

"Thank you, Ms Ryder. When you find the time, will you buy me male clothes?" He continued, trying to find a balance between asking and telling. "When you find the time, of course. I know how busy you are and your deadline." He added, trying to display his keenness that he was going to put her first and accept this latest development. However much he hated wearing the skirt. Did he hate it though? Was it that bad?

Ms Ryder considered what he had said for a moment.

"Yes of course, Amy. I am up against a deadline with the manuscript. I have an advance against a delivery date in one month's time. I'm still only on the first draft so I'll be working day and night. I'm rather snowed under. Once I find some daylight, I can look into your request. Give me time then we can maybe make a home delivery order."

She had agreed. Or had she? She said she would look into it. Did this mean she would get him male clothes or she would only think about it? She had said she would be busy. Snowed under. That meant a little longer dressed in skirts. And more teasing and sparring with Ellen, trying not to give her any excuses to cause problems.

Ellen returned and tossed a pair of black pantyhose at him. The moment with Ms Ryder was broken. He faked a smile at Ellen in thanks. He removed his shoes and pushed a foot into the tights and his big toe snagged. He took his foot out and tried again. It caught again.

Ms Ryder knelt by him. "Let me show you. There's a knack to this. All women know. You'll learn, Amy."

She rolled the pantyhose up and slipped it over his feet. She rolled it up his legs to above his knees. Goosebumps raised the hairs on the back of his neck and his skin tingled as her fingertips rubbed against his lower thighs.

"You can do the rest, Amy," She said as she stood up.

He was back down to earth and disappointed. He stood and pulled the pantyhose up and under his skirt and pushed his feet into the shoes. He was conscious of being watched by the approving looks of Ms Ryder and the barely disguised snarl of Ellen.

He brushed his skirt down with both hands. The skirt was soft and expensive feeling, like the clothes Anne Dufort had provided. Except these were clearly girls' clothes. It was a skirt. His penis expanded. The same as last night. He guessed it was a delayed reaction to Ms Ryder pulling the pantyhose up his legs. The touch of her fingers and the proximity of her face to his thighs were intoxicating. It couldn't be the excitement of wearing a skirt, that was certain. Wasn't it?

He wanted to hug Ms Ryder. She was kind. It was worth fighting for this job with her. It seemed she had forgiven his over-sleeping this morning. The skirt thing would be over before too long, a distant memory they would laugh about. They would joke about the time he had to wear a skirt because the lockdown prevented him from going home to get his own clothes.

For the time being, he would be on his guard continuously against Ellen. And her niece. Well, he said to himself, that's how it will be. It shouldn't be too hard now he knew what Ellen was up to.

Chapter 18 — Happy in Skirts

The next week passed without incident. He set the alarm on his phone for 6.30 am every morning, even at weekends. He had asked Ms Ryder for more skirts to wear. He hated doing it, but that was the plan. He'd show Ellen he wasn't concerned and she would never win. And he'd show Ms Ryder how accommodating he was.

Ms Ryder had been surprised and pleased at his request to wear other skirts. She happily provided him with more of her expensive, high-quality clothes. He hung them in the wardrobe in his room. Anyone who looked in there would have thought it was a woman's bedroom.

His approach was working. He got up and shaved and showered every morning and chose one of the plain skirts Ms Ryder had given him. He then selected a pretty top, black pantyhose and he wore the fat-heeled shoes.

Ms Ryder had also provided some shorter skirts in lighter colours and a box pleated skirt in grey. He wasn't sure why and he didn't imagine her ever wearing them. Jenny yes. Not Ms Ryder. Him neither.

She had given him a couple of dresses which also hung in the wardrobe. He had no intention of putting them on. He touched them all the same and they felt wonderful. Soft materials he had never experienced before. For a moment he thought about trying one on, to see how it looked, nothing more. He wondered what it might feel like to be inside a pretty dress. To walk around with it flowing around his legs, the low front, the shoulder straps. The thoughts made him flush with excitement. He supposed it must have been the thought of Ms Ryder wearing these clothes. That was it, he decided. What else could it be?

He opened the curtains and then the windows. It was now unseasonably warm, even this early in the year. The weather changed dramatically every day. He checked his phone and the forecast said 21 degrees C, nearly 70 Fahrenheit. He put the thick pantihose back and found a pack of thinner pantihose. They were a tan colour, thin, fine and smooth. There was a light sheen, and they glistened in the morning light. He had no option, the other tights would be far too hot when working around the house.

He slipped them on the way Fiona had shown meet last week, making sure they didn't snag. He looked at the other shoes Ms Ryder had lent him. They were on the rack at the bottom of the wardrobe. He spotted a tan coloured pair with thin heels, maybe two inches high. They attracted his attention as he thought they would go well with the tights. He took them out and turned them over in his hands. No, they were far too feminine.

He thought again. He could try them on, to see how they looked. A bit of fun, nothing more. He slipped them on and walked back and forth across his room. They clicked on the floorboards, a sound he enjoyed. *Click-clack, click-clack.* He found it was tricky to walk without being shaky and wobbly on the slimmer heels. After a few practices, he got the hang of it. More or less. Small steps and not too fast. And walk tall with confidence.

A light wind blew in from the open window and against his legs as he walked. The air swept around his legs; he felt light-headed. He guessed he must still be tired. The persistent erection he woke up with persisted. It was probably some kind of residual morning glory. The shoes went nicely with the pantyhose. His pantyhose. He saw a problem. The black hairs on his legs showed flat and squashed against the fine transparent nylons.

Anyway, he thought, the shoes were too feminine and probably impractical to work in.

He took them off with some reluctance and put on the black Mary Jane shoes and buckled them up. Plain, but far more practical. He looked at the wide black shoes on the end of his legs, a single black strap across both feet. Rounded shoes. They didn't go so well with the tan pantyhose as the slimmer, more elegant shoes he had tried. He could put on the thick black pantyhose. But it was going to be a warm day.

He took the Mary Janes off and put the tan shoes on again. They were far better. He stood and walked across the room a couple of times. They clicked and clacked in a more satisfactory way than the rubber heels of the Mary Janes. *Click-clack, click-clack, click-clack* on the floorboards. It was heady. The sandals looked, and felt, a hundred times better. The problem was they were so feminine. Problem? His feet were raised in the higher heel stretching his leg muscles, making them look taut and nicer. The muscle stretch was pleasant. His leg hairs, some flattened, a couple poking through the nylon were less attractive. There was nothing he could do about it.

He sat on the bed, the tan shoes on his feet. His leg muscles tingled, tight and firm. The shoes were slim and feminine. It was a wonderful feeling. He never imagined. He didn't want to be too feminine, the skirts and other female clothing were only a temporary solution, and plain. He should stick to them.

What would Ellen do? She had not been on his back recently. Would she be able to avoid making a comment? Call him a girly, or some other bad comment. What would Ms Ryder think? He couldn't decide what to do. He wanted to look tidy and well dressed for her. Maybe she would be angry, maybe not. Maybe she would be pleased he was well dressed?

He was frozen in indecision. He wanted to wear the shoes, but he didn't. The decision was taken out of his hands as he heard Ms Ryder calling from below and ringing her bell. She had heard him walking around the bedroom, his heels clicking on the floor. She shouted up to ask if he was ready and, if so, could he come down as she wanted breakfast earlier today. She added she had been up since 4 am working on her draft.

"Coming right now, Ms Ryder," he called back without thinking he had the higher heels on.

He went downstairs wobbling on the heels. He hadn't removed them in his haste. Too late, she had heard him coming and expected him right now. He couldn't go back and change now. He would go down and prepare the breakfast then return to change into the more practical shoes. He descended the stairs and went into the kitchen. His thin heels clipped on the tiled floor. *Click -lack, click-clack.* His stomach did a turn as the sound of his heels echoed around the hall. *Click-click, clack-clack.* Had he gone too far by putting on these feminine shoes? What had he been thinking? He thought about taking them off, walking in bare feet. He waited a moment in the hall. Ms Ryder wouldn't like bare feet.

She did insist on him being well-dressed. He looked down at the shoes and wiggled a foot in the air. They were nicer with the lighter pantyhose. Maybe it was better. He would tell her he was changing back to the Mary Jane's.

He saw his leg hairs, thick and black though the thinner nylon. It wasn't his fault he had no trousers to wear. It was Ellen's, she had shrunk his only pair of trousers. No, if he had hairy legs, then so be it.

He went into the kitchen and made Ms Ryder some toast, prepared grapefruit and made coffee. He carried it to her office on a tray. He kept the shoes on, better than bare feet. He went to Fiona's office and the door was closed. He balanced the tray in one hand and knocked and went in after she had told him to enter. He trotted in, feeling like a show pony in the higher thinner heels. He placed the tray on her desk.

She instantly straightened it to line up with her keyboard.

Ms Ryder looked away from her screen, eyes drawn and red. She rubbed an eye with the heel of her hand. Far from looking bad, she looked beautiful and vulnerable. He wanted to do whatever he could to make her life easier.

"Thank you, Amy." She sat back in her office chair and picked up her coffee mug. She took a long sip and the caffeine instantly softened her tired face.

He nodded a rapid acknowledgement, more of a head movement than a bow. He wobbled unsteadily to the door. His walk attracted Fiona's attention.

"Amy, come back here."

He turned back. Her eyes fell to his shoes. He looked away, embarrassed.

"Is the toast done OK, Ms Ryder," he said trying to avoid the conversation he knew was coming.

She put her hands on her lap. She was wearing a black leather skirt which was raised above her knee as she sat. A shaft of sunlight flitted in through the windows behind her. Several birds, perched unseen in an apple tree chirped in chorus.

"The shoes, the tights," she said.

He flinched then looked up at her, his chin low on his chest. His legs were like jelly and his cheeks flushed. The room was silent.

"Yes?" he said in a failed attempt at sounding casual.

"I like them, good choice. They go nicely with the lighter tights, also a great choice," she said.

"Thank you, Ms Ryder, I thought they might be better in the warmer weather and the black shoes didn't go."

"Good decision, Amy. Well done."

"I'll change them in a moment I wanted to try them, then you wanted breakfast early, but I realise they're not appropriate."

He turned to leave and got halfway to the door. He wanted to escape from this humiliation, to hide away. It wasn't that she was making fun of him, or forcing him to dress as a girl.

"They are appropriate. Keep them on. I like them."

This wasn't what he had expected. He was caught. She wanted him to remain in something even more feminine. He thought he might faint with embarrassment. He went to leave.

"Stop."

He froze like a statue. *What now?*

"The tights."

He turned back. He didn't know what she meant. She had praised his choice of pantihose. *Perhaps they were twisted?*

"I can see your leg hairs through them. It's very untidy."

His head dropped. "I'm, I'm, I'm sorry. I'll g-go upstairs and change them for the thick ones. It's what I planned to do"

He looked up and she was smiling sweetly. "No, Amy, they are lovely, perfect for this weather. No, I have a much better idea. Wait here."

She picked up her mobile phone and flicked a finger on the screen, touched it and put it inside her hair and against an ear. The tinny sound of ringing sounded out, mingling with the bird chirps from outside.

"Hello, where are you?" she asked into the phone, all the time watching him. She listened. "Great, can you come to my office now. I have a little job for you."

She clicked the phone off and placed it back on the desk. She placed her hands back on her laps and waited. He didn't want to know who was coming, but he had a nasty feeling he knew already.

A minute or two later, Ellen burst into the room. David knew whatever was coming next was not going to be good for him. Not one bit.

Chapter 19 — Shaved and Smooth

"Thank you for coming so quickly, Ellen. We have a small problem. Amy is using thinner tights, but her leg hairs show though which is so untidy." She closed her eyes a moment and shook her head as if he were a naughty, but much-loved child. "I do hate untidy things."

Ellen looked him up and down, her eyes resting on his legs and then his slim shoes. "Isn't *she* the pretty one."

He cringed at her emphasis on *she*. Ms Ryder tapped Ellen playfully.

"Stop teasing him, Ellen." She put on a fake frown. "Can you see the problem, Ellen?"

Ellen's stare remained fixed on his legs. "Yes. She has hairy legs, not very girl-like Fiona." A hand went to her chin. "I have an electric lady shaver in the spare bedroom for when I stay over. I can remove the hair, it shouldn't take too long."

David picked at one of his bitten down nails. *Shave? Legs?* His mind raced. He had to keep up the pretence all was fine with wearing female clothes until Ms Ryder had completed her draft. Shaving his legs sounded like one step closer to being more feminine. He needed to delay things.

He had an idea. "It's not a problem, I can change into thicker pantyhose to hide the hairs. Besides, I'll be back in trousers in a couple of weeks, so there's no need to drag Ellen away from her work."

There was a pause. Then Ellen spoke. "It's not a problem, Amy. I'll shave your legs for you. I'd be happy to." Her grin was wide and sinister, her teeth bared.

"Of course. Thank you, Ellen," said Ms Ryder.

He took a half step away from them. He had been outwitted again. Anger welled up, he had to swallow it back. Keep things on an even keel and keep his job, he told himself. Once he was back in male clothing, all would be fine.

Ellen's grin was still spread over her face. "I can show Amy the technique. She can shave herself the next time. To keep her body smooth and feminine like a good girl."

He winced at her taunts, openly using feminine pronouns when talking about him: *she* and *herself*. And calling him a *girl*. Ms Ryder appeared to not notice, or be bothered by it. She was more interested in getting the dispute cleared up rather than any derision aimed at him by her long-term employee and friend.

"I'm so pleased you two are getting along, I was worried at first. But now it's all going well." She smiled happily.

David nodded sullenly with a sense of doom. Ellen remained impassive. Her mind was elsewhere, it was clear she was revelling in getting one over on him yet again. The decision was made; his legs were to be shaved and Ellen was going to be doing it. He had no choice in the matter. No choice in what happens to his own body.

With a sense of his total impotence and a mounting gloom, he allowed Ellen to lead him from Ms Ryder's office. Fiona's instructions rang out as they left: d*o whatever Ellen tells you to do Amy.* He was certain this was not going to go well for him. He felt as if he was falling down a deep well, spinning out of control. Every moment he was closer to the bottom where growing femininity awaited.

He knew this latest step into femininity was his fault. His fault for putting on thinner pantyhose and the pretty shoes. And his fault for feeling good in them. The thought didn't help his mood as we went to the kitchen. Ellen told him to sit and remove his shoes and tights while she went to get the electric lady shaver.

He complied as if he were in a dream. Fiona had been right; his legs didn't look good with hairs showing through the tights. How could he have been so stupid? How could he have liked the femininity of the tights and shoes? He thought Fiona would like the thinner pantyhose, but all it had done was highlight his leg hairs. As he sat, his skirt hung across his thighs; it was a nice fresh feeling, he had to admit to himself. Again. What was going on?

Approaching footsteps from the hall announced the imminent reappearance of Ellen. She entered the room, electric shaver in hand, face set in a look of pleasure. She plugged in the shaver.

With pursed lips and a cruel grin, Ellen knelt at his feet. She switched on the hand-held machine, the metallic buzz sounded like an angry wasp trapped in a glass bowl to David's ears. She started on his lower legs and calves before moving above his knees, the cutter going up and down and around in circles. Dark hairs fell to the floor tiles; his masculinity was being visibly emasculated and falling in small heaps on the floor.

Ellen told him to sit on the edge of the chair. She forced his legs apart and manoeuvred between them. She pushed his skirt up so it was just covering his panties. The first stirrings of an erection threatened, her hands and face were now six inches or so from his penis. If she was bothered in any way, it didn't show. David began to sweat. He was bothered.

"I can do my own thighs, Ellen. You don't need to worry." His voice came out high, nervous.

"I'm not worried." She pushed his legs apart as far as they would comfortably go and slid the shaver up the inside of his crotch, grazing against his growing penis inside the small stretched panties.

"No," he protested. "I think it better if I did it."

He put a hand against the side of his balls to shield them from the shaver and her hand. With his other hand, he pulled his skirt hem down to cover his expanding panty bulge.

Ellen took her hands away. She sighed extravagantly.

"Fiona wants your legs clean of hair and Fiona told me to do it for you."

She leant back on her haunches and one hand went to a broad hip, the other hand was still wrapped around the small shaver. The thin white lead trailed along the red-tiled floor to the plug socket.

"Shall I go and tell her you're not cooperating?" She put her head to one side.

He didn't want that, not if his plan was to succeed. He had to continue being cooperative and accept whatever was thrown at him.

"No, I don't want you to tell her." He spoke in a hushed beaten tone.

He had been checkmated again by Ellen. He couldn't go against Ms Ryder's wishes he look more tidy, but to agree was to become more feminine. It wasn't unpleasant to be wearing female clothes, on the contrary, it was liberating. And not a little erotic. But, he knew it wasn't right. A man should not be dressed in a skirt and have shaved legs. More relevant, he knew Ellen was pushing his descent into femininity to make him snap and resign from the job. To let her niece Jenny in. And Ellen was getting the better of him at every turn. She was winning.

Ellen brought him out of his thoughts by shoving his skirt back up his legs. This time she fully exposed his panties and his erect bulge. She put the shaver back on his thigh and looked directly at the lump pushing against the white cotton panties.

"Well, my, my. What do we have here?" She said. "I hope you're not going to play with it again."

He put his head down in shame at the thought.

She held the shaver against his skin, still not flipping the on switch. "Your little winky is excited. I can see you like being a girly."

He didn't answer her. He grabbed the side of the chair with both arms and looked away from what was going on. His teeth gritted together and he closed his eyes. The buzzing of the shaver came back on and he felt the cool metal of the cutting edge flow over his delicate thigh skin. It was like the sound of a dentist drilling into a bad tooth. Except he hated himself for enjoying the extraction of his masculinity.

"O.M.G." A girl's voice screamed out. "He's got a boner."

Chapter 20 — Damp Patches

His eyes popped open instantly. Jenny, Ellen's niece, was in the kitchen, he hadn't heard her come in over the sound of the electric razor. Her eyes were wide, a hand clamped over her mouth, long pink nails digging into her cheeks. Her honey-blond hair curled around her face, small pert breasts outlined against a pink woollen jumper. She was in a tiny white ra-ra skirt and her long false eyelashes blinked rapidly.

Ellen continued shaving his inner thigh. "Fiona asked me to shave Amy's legs. They were all nasty and hairy."

She finished one thigh and moved to the other. Jenny was giggling girlishly through her hand.

"That's awesome, auntie." She leant in towards his exposed panties and the bulge. "Auntie Ellen, he likes that. He's got a raging stiffy."

For reasons he couldn't begin to understand, this only served to make his erection harder. Ellen had completed almost all the shaving and moved her hand up to the area between his genitals and leg. The shaver vibrated against his balls, the back of her had rubbed against his erection. She held it there for longer than he thought necessary. Jenny moved in even closer to look at the bulge in his panties, her smokey made-up eyes a couple of inches away.

"Auntie Ellen, he's gotta damp spot on his panties." She looked closer then jerked her head back. "It's *jizz*. He's got some *pre-jizz* leaking out. That's *mank*. Urghhh." Her face creased into an exaggerated look of disgust. She put her tongue out and pretended to retch.

He had leaked pre-cum. A circular darker damp stain had spread over his stark white panties, where the end of his penis was. He looked at it in abject horror.

Ellen recoiled. "Don't you dare cum again." She stood up and backed away. "Disgusting." Her face pinched and horrified. She stood next to Jenny. "I've caught her masturbating in her room already."

This couldn't get any worse. To his surprise, Jenny backed down and sat beside his legs with her back to him. He didn't understand what she was doing. The back of her head moved towards his thigh, keeping his legs wide open. Her hair felt erotic against his skin, some hair flowed over his erection. This was not normal.

There was a flash and a click. Jenny stood up, turned and showed him her phone screen. She had taken a selfie of her grinning at his bulge and panty stain. His face was out of the picture. He made a grab at the phone, but she jerked it away and he flailed at thin air.

"I have to post this so my *besties* can see this, they won't believe it."

Her apparent disgust of a few moments ago was now dissipated by the thought of her friends' social media comments on her photo. He pulled his skirt down to cover the offending stain and straining erection. He didn't know where to look or what to do. The situation was out of control.

"Take your panties off." Ellen was standing, with hands on hips, looking down on me.

"I will not." He snapped back.

She looked to the ceiling. Jenny's unblinking eyes swivelled between me and Ellen, her eyes like saucers since she arrived.

"Cum smells, even the dribble you've discharged. You wouldn't want Fiona complaining that you smell of damp semen, would you?"

She was right. Ellen held out a hand. She wiggled her fingers to indicate that he get a move on. He supposed it made little difference if he removed them under his skirt as his erection would be hidden. He slipped them off, holding on the hem of his skirt and he held them out to her. Ellen grimaced again and took them on the edge between two fingers held out at arm's length.

"Yuk. Gross." Jenny said. Her legs were bare and her skirt was so short, the slightest movement should have shown her panties. Somehow they remained hidden to him.

Ellen marched to the utility area with his panties, holding them away, the look of disgust written on her face. She called out for him to put his stockings and shoes back on. He did as he was told. The stockings looked much nicer on his smooth hairless legs. Ms Ryder had been correct. She usually was.

He heard Ellen opening the washing machine door then slamming it shut afterwards. As she returned to the kitchen, Ms Ryder called out for him. She wanted him to do something for her.

"It's back to work girly boy," Ellen said.

He didn't even have time to put on a fresh pair of panties. He hoped his hard-on would go down quickly. It was tenting out the front of his skirt.

Chapter 21 — Accustomed to Femininity

For the next two days, Ellen pretended to be friendly with him whenever Ms Ryder was around. When she wasn't, she called him names: panty-boy or girly, sissy-girl. Her jibes were meant to hurt. Ms Ryder, on the other hand, seemed pleased with his work. She did insist on calling him Amy now and was pleased his legs were smooth under the stockings.

She mentioned his hair was becoming untidy. Unlike for his legs, she had been far too busy to worry. It was true it was getting long and unkempt. It was longer than he had ever worn it. It fell over his shoulders and down the top of his back. It was thick, but it hung limp. He had started washing it every day and made sure it was combed and this had seemed to make it acceptable for her. Up to now.

He now had to shave his legs every day. That was now the rule. He loved the feel of the smooth legs and the feeling inside his stockings. Thankfully, Ms Ryder told Ellen to give him her electric lady shaver so he was able to do it himself and not have to suffer any further humiliation of having Ellen doing it, with Jenny watching.

The other change was Ms Ryder preferred him in light stockings and the higher heeled shoes. She told him to wear them every day. She said she expected her personal assistant to look business-like and well-dressed. He was certainly well dressed, the trouble was it was in female clothes.

Ms Ryder added her social media activities to his role. She scheduled an 8 am meeting for fifteen minutes every day with what she wanted to say to her followers. He took notes in a pad, in his black skirt, stockings and heels and blouse.

Two weeks after the incident with Ellen and Jenny in the kitchen, he was preparing coffee and toast for Ms Ryder. He looked out across the garden. The early morning low-hanging mist was lifting. The day promised to be sunny.

He put the coffee and breakfast on a tray and went through to Ms Ryder's office for the now regular morning briefing. He knocked and entered. She wasn't at her desk as she usually was. She was sitting on the office sofa opposite her desk, an arm across the back, her legs crossed. She tapped the place next to her twice with a flat hand. He placed the tray on her coffee table and sat down, keeping his legs together and bent away. She smiled and looked at them.

"Amy, you look wonderful. I don't understand why there are girl styles and man styles. Why can't all males look like you? Pretty.

He blushed deeply, unsure if he liked the compliment or not. "Thank you, Ms Ryder, but it's only until you've completed your manuscript and can find the time to get me some male clothing."

She sat up. Her face turned serious. "Yes, yes, the manuscript. "It's done and ready to go to the editors."

"Oh," he replied, momentarily surprised. The moment had finally arrived. He felt a strange tang of disappointment. He brushed a hand against his skirt, the smooth shiny material soft and sensuous.

She touched his arm. "I thought you'd be pleased."

"Yes, yes of course I am. I'm happy for you, Ms Ryder."

He was relieved at the thought of returning to male clothing but with an overwhelming sense of the end of an era of some kind.

Ms Ryder sat back again and looked dreamy. "It's a great weight off my mind. I had a deadline to meet and now this millstone has been lifted." She retreated into thought. "Millstone lifted?" She thought again. "Oh dear, writers should never use such common clichés. What a disaster I am at times." She brightened up.

He was enjoying spending relaxed time with her after seeing her so stressed and committed to her work. And after some of his early mistakes, he felt he had proved to her he could be an effective assistant. He thought this might be the moment to press the question of her ordering him new clothing. Male clothing. He was beginning to worry about his acceptance of the overtly female clothing he was wearing, let alone shaving his legs. He tried to tell himself it was all a plan to thwart Ellen. But he knew this wasn't entirely true.

"So you'll now have the time to get me my new clothing? This afternoon?"

She looked back at him, a confused look across her eyes and forehead. Her eyebrows lifted as if she had thought of something.

"Oh Amy, I had completely forgotten about that. I have become accustomed to you dressed as a girl. It seemed so natural for you."

This wasn't the response he'd expected. He had to press on. "But I thought we'd agreed that once your manuscript was finished, you would look into getting me some appropriate clothing." He began to feel uncomfortable, fearful she was about to go back on her words.

She shook her head slightly, she appeared to be disappointed. "I happen to think your current clothing is entirely appropriate. I don't see what the problem is." She paused to reflect on the conversation. "But yes, I did promise to look into purchasing you male clothing. A commitment is a commitment, however unnecessary the commitment may be."

Her lack of concern at him being dressed as a female worried him. She had said she would get him the new clothing, so he pushed on. "Shall we order it now? I see your computer is on."

She waved a hand in the air. "In time, Amy in time."

He waited with a sense of apprehension. "So when, Ms Ryder?"

She snorted in frustration. "We have something else to sort out first. That's the focus of our little morning briefing today. Then we can cosider new clothes for you but it's not my priority if I'm honest. I happen to think you look lovely as you are and you need to get out of the mindset about what are male clothes."

He wasn't getting out of female clothes today, that was clear. Ms Ryder lifted her coffee mug, took a small taste and put it back on the tray.

"My agent, Louise Lipman, is coming for dinner this evening." She sat back and looked down guiltily. "Yes I know there's a lockdown, but she lives in the village and we have no virus cases anywhere in the area. It's wrong to break the lockdown, but in this case, I think it's safe enough, just the once. She'll be staying overnight."

He went to speak and Fiona cut him off.

"It will be a business meal. We'll be discussing the next stages for my book. Professional editing, proofing, design and formatting and finally, marketing. That kind of stuff. It's better in person than on Zoom or Skype or whatever"

His stomach turned. Someone else was coming to the house and he was still dressed in a skirt. He had become used to appearing in female clothes in front of Ms Ryder, Ellen and now Jenny. But another person was being introduced to his femininity. Ms Ryder noticed his discomfort. She tapped him on one of his nylon covered knees.

"Don't worry about Louise, I have a plan. She won't be concerned about you because I will make sure you will look lovely."

"I'm sorry, Ms Ryder, but I am worried. She'll see I'm a man in female clothing. I'll be so embarrassed, it's humiliating for me. It's bad enough dressing like this in front of you and Ellen. Maybe I can spend the evening in my room."

"Oh no, Amy. You need to be there. Apart from serving us, you need to hear what we decide. As my personal assistant, some of the tasks will be for you to perform. I want you involved."

She looked pleased with herself. David put his hands on his forehead, then ran his fingers back through his hair pulling it tight. Ms Ryder put a hand on his knee again, this time keeping it there. Her touch felt like a tang of electricity in the shape of her fingers on his skin.

"But don't worry," she said. "I've thought about this. You look lovely, but maybe it's unfair on her to present a man in female clothing. I see no reason for men not to look like girls or be feminine, but she's old fashioned. I don't want her distracted. She needs to focus on my work."

He agreed enthusiastically that she didn't need to see a man in female clothing. Then he realised he didn't know what he was agreeing to.

"You need to wear something better for this evening. You wear these same rather plain clothes every day. Black skirt and white top. Great for working, not so good for a business dinner. Or for serving us."

This sounded more positive to him, apart from the serving bit, but he accepted this was part of the job.

"Yes of course," he said, still not sure what she had in mind.

She closed her eyes for a moment, as though concentrating on her plans for her meeting with Louise Lipman. David wondered what clothes she would find for him to wear for the evening. Maybe she had a grey suit with trousers? Maybe something dark blue? It would be something she hadn't given him yet to wear, he guessed, as it was undoubtedly expensive. He was sure she was going to lend him something special. He could not meet Louise Lipman dressed like a girl.

Her eyes sprung open. "There's so much to get done today before Louise arrives."

"So what will I be wearing, Ms Ryder? One of your business trouser suits?"

She stared into his eyes, her laughter lines creased in pleasure. "Oh no, Amy. I have a much better idea than that."

Chapter 22 — Disguised as a Girl

David wondered what her idea could be.

Ms Ryder wrinkled her nose. "I'm going to ask Ellen to help you find something suitable from hers or Julie's clothing. I'm sure they will be only too happy to help. You're all getting on so well."

He was sure Ellen would be happy to find another reason to humiliate him. It had been a while and she had seemed to be sulking. His body slumped as if pushed down by an invisible weight. He did not trust Ellen, or her stupid niece, to have his best interests in mind. Seeing his discomfort, she touched his cheek.

"What we're going to do is put you in disguise. It was Ellen's idea, to be honest."

"Disguise?" he asked warily.

"Yes. Disguised as a girl. You've been wearing a skirt for some time, so a more elegant dress or skirt will not be a problem for you. Your feminine clothes will look unusual with your male face. I also realise you probably won't have much of a clue what to put on, so Ellen will help."

She beamed a wide smiled. She thought this was a great idea. He didn't like it one bit.

"I've already agreed it all with Ellen and that young niece of hers, they will choose some nice clothes for you. They said they are happy to loan you some of their things. They have offered to do your makeup and hair. Ellen said once they had finished with you, Louise will never notice you're not a real girl." She folded her arms, a content expression across her face. "Yes, they were Ellen's exact words."

He stood up. Then sat down again. He was shocked and his mind turned over and over.

"No, that's not necessary, Ms Ryder. Thank you for thinking about me. But I don't want to put them to any trouble. I'm sure Ellen is very busy."

"Nonsense," she said cheerfully. "They said they would love to do this."

Yes, he thought, I bet they would.

Ms Ryder ran a finger through his long hair.

"You're going to look so pretty, Amy. Louise will never realise you're a man after Ellen and

Jenny have finished with you. There will be nothing to worry about."

He put his face in his hands. This was spinning out of control. His policy of appeasement was falling apart. He had plenty to worry about.

Chapter 23 — Accentuate the Femininity

The early afternoon was dull and gloomy when Ellen and Jenny came for him. They led him up to his bedroom. The two ladies were carrying a suitcase which they said was full of pretty clothes, makeup and lots of girly things. They led him up to his bedroom, giggling and chatting like two schoolgirls. He heard them chatting about how they had dragged the suitcase across the field.

Ellen was dressed in black leggings. Jenny was in a tiny leather brown pencil skirt that was little more than a belt. Her false eyelashes blinked regularly, her red lipstick was bright and luminous.

They stripped him down to a pair of small yellow panties. He was deflated. They told him to shower but not to wash his hair. He went to the shower in a daze and closed the door behind him. He removed his panties and showered. He didn't like where this was going.

He dried and put the panties back on, he didn't want them teasing him about his penis. Outside, a rumble of thunder groaned and dark clouds covered the sun. He heard the first spots of rain began spattering on the roof.

He opened the shower room door. Ellen pushed him back in, Jenny followed with a plastic chair.

"Sit," Ellen ordered.

They draped a towel around his neck. Jenny held a plastic bottle which she up-ended and squeezed gel-like liquid into his hair. He tried to stand up. Ellen pushed him down by his shoulders.

"What...?" He started to ask.

Her voice came from behind him. "We're covering up your grey hairs which have been coming up in your roots. Don't worry. Girls don't show their grey hairs so we need to do this so your disguise is complete."

"But..." He began, straightening up.

"Relax girly, we're hiding your grey hairs."

He sat back. Jenny rubbed the gel in as if she was shampooing. He closed his eyes as she massaged his scalp, enjoying the sensation and being pampered a little. Her fingers soothed his tension. Ellen told him to wait where he was for thirty minutes and they went downstairs.

Half an hour later, they came back and put his head under the shower and rinsed the hair dye away. He watched as mauve dye washed down the plughole. He enjoyed Jenny's fingers rubbing and massaging his scalp, her breasts pushing against his back.

They returned to the main bedroom, the towel still around his neck. Jenny carried the plastic chair in and he sat down. Jenny blow-dried his hair with a large black dryer and he closed his eyes again to enjoy the attention. This was not so bad, he thought. She brushed his fringe forward over his face. He heard the snipping sound of scissors in front of his face and snapped his eyes open.

"We're tidying your style up a little at the front." Ellen was standing watching Jenny.

He supposed this was fine and closed his eyes again to enjoy the attention. Jenny finished, he felt her fluffing his fringe and he opened his eyes. She was kneeling in front of him. She took one of his hands. She picked up a small bottle with a pink liquid inside.

It was nail varnish. She was going to paint his fingernails. Pink. He pulled his hands under his thighs.

Ellen's face wrinkled in annoyance. "How are we supposed to disguise you as a girl if you have plain male nails? Answer me?"

Jenny took one of his hands and he let her take it. Ellen was correct, he needed this disguise. One last night of humiliation and he would return to male clothes. One more test.

Jenny painted his nails on both hands. They were a bright shocking pink.

"Why do they have to be so pink, Ellen?" he asked. He had allowed them to do it without a fight; he felt guilty.

"We need to accentuate the girliness, Amy. Your nails and clothes need to be more girly than say, mine or Fiona's. Maybe not Jenny's. Because we're real females it's obvious we're women. You need a lot more work." She lifted one of his hands and looked satisfied. "Although not as much work to look like a girl as many men would."

That stung him, although he was also trying to work out what *accentuate* meant. He wondered why everyone he met spoke as if they had swallowed a dictionary. He gave up thinking and snatched his hand away petulantly. Ellen appeared unconcerned. She and Jenny were now more interested in the clothes they had brought into his room.

They were picking up various items of clothing, discussing, giggling.

"Put this on first, Amy." Ellen held out a yellow bra that matched the panties he was in.

He stared at her in disgust. "I'm not putting a bra on."

Ellen went behind him. She put the bra to his chest. "Nonsense, Amy, girls need bras. And since Fiona said we have to disguise you as a girl, you need a bra. Do you want me to go and see her to explain how you're not co-operating?"

He tried to think of a come-back line, but before anything came to mind, she clipped the bra on around his chest.

Ellen appraised the bra. "Good girl."

Jenny sniggered.

Ellen retrieved a frilly white belt with straps hanging loose. It was a suspender belt.

"I don't need this Ellen, I have tights and hold-ups."

She shook her head. "Tut, tut, Amy. Feminine? Girly? Pretty? Remember? *Ac-cen-tu-ate?*"

He opened his mouth to debate whether Fiona wanted him very girly. He didn't remember Fiona putting it in those terms. She had said he needed to be well-disguised.

Ellen pulled him to stand up from under his arms; clipped on the suspender belt and the thin straps hung against his thin pale thighs, small red bows on the end of each one. There was a larger red bow on the front of the belt which was tight around his stomach.

"Sit on the bed, Amy, there's a good girl." Ellen pointed to the end of the bed.

"Stop calling me a girl, Ellen."

She ignored him as he sat down as ordered anyway. He understood there was sense to what Ms Ryder wanted. It was for a one-off event and it will help to get her book completed. It would allow him to return to being a male. He didn't feel nasty wearing female clothing and being more careful with his looks, it all made sense. It was more that it wasn't right wearing girls' clothes. He told himself he was a man and men didn't wear skirts. It's wrong. Nice, but wrong. An interesting diversion for a short period of his life. He considered he might incorporate it into a sex game with a future girlfriend. Yes, it was a good idea. There was something exciting about it. Maybe he'd look up Olga again.

His toes tickled which pulled him out of his self-absorbed thoughts. Jenny was kneeling at his feet painting pink varnish onto one of his big toes. He pulled his foot away without thinking.

Ellen stood over him, frustration written on her face.

"Amy, you are not helping here. We're trying to follow Fiona's instructions." She breathed in. "Do you want Louise Lipman to see you as a man dressed as a girl?"

His head dropped. "No, Ellen. But..."

"Then let us get on with our work. We know what we're doing."

Jenny pulled his foot back and continued painting his toenails the same luminous pink as his fingernails. Ellen leant over and made up his face. He felt the light tickle of a brush on his eyelashes and then something being dabbed on his cheeks. She put lipstick on his lips.

She stood back and admired her work.

"My, my. I believe you're going to pass. Are you sure you're not really a girl, Amy?"

Chapter 24 — The Feminine Exhibit

Once they had finished with the make-up and nail varnish, Ellen told him to hold his hands and feet out to let the varnish dry. She then dried it with the hairdryer. Ellen got up and came back with a blouse on a hanger. It was lavender with frills down the front along the buttons and buttonholes. He was relieved it wasn't a garish yellow or in a luminous pink like his nails. He stood and let them slip it on over his bra and then they buttoned it up. Both the women smiled constantly as they worked on him.

Jenny checked the nail polish was dry and knelt again and pushed on fine skin-coloured stockings over his feet. She pulled them up his legs and to the top of his thighs. Her blond hair brushed his smooth legs and he felt her nails against his skin as she pulled the nylons up.

Her fingers brushed against his penis, tucked inside the flimsy thin panties. His penis was already stiff as she clipped the stockings to his suspender belt. She did the same for his other leg and he then had a firm erection. Jenny's head was inches away as she worked attaching the stockings to the suspender. She couldn't avoid but see his panties bursting out like a tent,

"Ooh," she squealed with delight. She poked it with a long red nail. "She's got a little stiffy again." She looked over at Ellen. "I hope she doesn't dribble into her panties like last time, Auntie Ellen."

He groaned and Ellen snorted a laugh. He wanted to be covered instead of standing in stockings, suspender belt and small fine panties with a bulge at the front. He would at this moment gratefully put on a skirt to cover his embarrassment. His erection was outlined against the thin panties. He placed both hands over it. Jenny got up and went to the pile of clothes and other items. She walked back with a pair of white high-heeled sandals swinging on one finger. They had a single strap around the ankle area and two parallel straps across the front. The worst part was they were around four inches high. She laid them at his feet.

He looked at the sandals like they were two unexploded bombs. "How do you expect me to walk in those?"

"You'll get used to it. Put them on." Ellen's voice was firm. "You're going to practice with us."

He placed one foot then the other into the sandals. Jenny did up the straps around his heels. He stood and tried to balance on the heels, feeling vulnerable, as if he were on a pedestal with his new femininity exhibited.

He asked to put on something to cover his panties and the erection. Ellen barked at him, telling him to try walking. She didn't want to know. He walked towards the door, his hands remaining over his stubborn erection. Ellen pulled them away.

"You need your arms for balancing, not touching yourself up. Now, smaller steps are the key to walking like a girl. Again. Walk."

He walked to the other side of the room, his tented panties leading the way, sweat beading on his brow. The heels *click-clacking* on the floorboards as before. It was beyond humiliation. He made his steps smaller, hoping once he got it right he could cover up the offending bulge in his panties. His calves were tight in their unnatural position. He found after some practice, he could walk, if he was careful. If he took it slowly.

"Right, not perfect, but it will have to do. Let's cover up this awful boner of yours, it's not very feminine, is it." Ellen sniggered.

For once he agreed about something with Ellen. About being covered up, not being feminine.

As he turned by the wall from his final practice walk, he saw Jenny was holding a hanger with a pink skirt. His eyes widened in horror. It was a power-pink mini with sharp pencil pleats. It couldn't have been more than eight inches long. Maybe shorter. The skirt swung in her hands and she shimmied the light cotton material from one side to the other.

"I can't wear that," he said. "This is a business meeting."

Ellen took it from Jenny and shoved it into his chest. "This is what you'll be wearing, girlie. Put it on."

He kept his hands at his side. "That's enough Ellen," he said, raising his voice. "I know what you're up to."

Their eyes locked.

"You're pushing me until I snap and walk out, leaving my job vacant for Jenny."

He stamped a foot and toppled which made the two women laugh.

"I'm not going to give in. I'm going to tell Ms Ryder what you're trying to do. She wanted me disguised as a girl, I understand. But, she also wanted me to look professional, not dressed in a micro skirt. Like a slut. A bimbo."

He waited for their reaction. Ellen raised her eyebrows. With a swift movement, she grabbed him and sat on the bed, pulling him onto her lap. She pulled down his panties and a *slap* came down on his bare buttocks. He was too shocked to react. *Slap*, another spank across his buttocks. He felt the imprint of her hand on his bum cheeks. *Slap*, another.

He went to get up and she pushed his head back.

"Are you going to put on the pretty pink skirt or shall I spank you some more?"

He touched his bare bottom. It was warm and stung smarted. He did not want her doing that again. Not only did it hurt, but he was sprawled over her knee. He felt like a naughty schoolboy.

She allowed him to get off and fumble with his panties to cover his erection.

"I'm going to discuss this with Ms Ryder right now," he said.

Ellen raised her eyebrows. "Be my guest, Amy. You're going to go and see Fiona dressed in a flimsy pair of panties with a raging erection?"

He looked down. His erection was pushing the panties away from his groin. He saw the base of his penis and his pubic hairs. His balls peeked out from either side on the thin cotton. He couldn't go downstairs to talk to Fiona, not like this.

He grabbed the little skirt from Jenny's grasp and pulled it on.

"Right. Now I can go."

Jenny dragged the body-length mirror over and positioned it in front of David.

He rocked back in shock. His eyes ran up from the high thin stilettos, the shiny stockings, his skirt hanging across bare skin around the upper part of white thighs. The stocking tops were below the short hem, frilly against the powder pink of the neat pleats. The suspender clasps were in clear view. His face was made up. He saw a pretty girl. His hair had dried into a much lighter shade of blonde than a mere tint. It was light blond. He thought he might faint. They had died it a lighter blond.

"You're ready, girly. You can show Fiona."

Ellen tried to look calm then exploded into laughter.

Chapter 25 — Never Too Girly

He felt faint. It had to be the stress, it couldn't be the emotion and feelings of this light, flowing miniskirt against his legs.

He stamped down the stairs awkwardly and into Ms Ryder's office without knocking. She was typing intently, eyes fixed on the screen of her laptop. She said nothing. He stopped, suddenly feeling stupid.

"Ms Ryder?"

She continued to study her screen. "Don't you knock now, Amy?"

He had gone too far in his anger and forgotten the etiquette she demanded. He should have known she was busy, she was always being meticulous in her work. He had disturbed her, something she had made clear he must not do from the beginning. That's what his job was; to make sure she suffered no disruption and now he was causing it. Ellen had wound him up like a child's clockwork toy and then let him go. To go and prove he wasn't up to the job. She was outwitting him in every area. He had over-reacted, as she wanted.

Well, he decided, he had got this far and now she was disrupted. He thought he might as well press on.

"I'm s, s, sorry Ms Ryder. But, but, I think Ellen has gone too far this time."

He waited for a response. She continued typing and was fixed on what was on her screen.

He continued in the face of her disinterest. "Look what they've done to me. I can't wear this. I can't look like this. Please do something, Ms Ryder. Ellen and Jenny are trying to make me look silly."

She typed and stared at the screen.

She huffed a sigh. "Amy. Ellen's been with me for years, I trust her, she's a confident and friend. I've left your disguise as a girl for her to sort out. I have the utmost confidence she'll do what's best. Now go back upstairs and leave me to complete my preparations; do whatever she tells you."

She finally turned away from the screen to look at me. She stared straight into my face, not taking in what I was wearing.

"Get back upstairs and let her finish what she was doing and do not disrupt me like this ever again, Amy. Because if you do, it will be the last time, believe me."

She swivelled back on her chair and went back to work. He stood a moment feeling even more stupid. There was a catch in his throat, this was going to be Ellen's way or no way. He had to choose and quickly. What options did he have? If he refused to go disguised as a girl, he was going to lose the job and Ellen would win. If he remained as a girly girl, he would keep his job and Ellen will have humiliated him. It seemed as if Ellen wins both ways. But maybe not? If he kept his job, Ellen will be unable to put Jenny in the role which was her prime motive for his humiliation. He had to see this though, dressed as a girl. It was the best of two bad options.

He dipped a small curtsy. Ms Ryder didn't notice; he said sorry and left her office. He had to go through with this deception. That meant he wins.

He went back up to his bedroom. He was going to lose this battle, but he was going to win the war.

Chapter 26 — Meeting the Mistress

It was early evening and David was waiting by the front door to greet Louise Lipman. When he had returned with his tail between his legs earlier, Ellen and Jenny put some finishing touches to his appearance.

They combed out his hair so it was thick and straight. Jenny had blow-dried the ends into an extravagant curl which bounced as one piece as he walked on his four-inch heels. The powder-pink pleated skirt was much too short for his comfort. It was no more than an inch below the bulge in his tiny panties. Two small crescents of bum cheeks protruded at the back. The lack of comfort was also due to having a raging erection which threatened to pop out of his tiny panties and lift the front of the light skirt. His erection was held back by a tiny triangle of cotton that would struggle to hold it in if he had been flaccid. He was not flaccid.

Ellen had packed his bra with panties to give the appearance of real breasts. They had thinned his eyebrows.

He stared down at the floor. Louise Lipman had called to say she was five minutes away. Ms Ryder had told him that, as her assistant, he should answer the door. The pink nail varnish screamed out from his toes through the fine stockings and the open toes of the white sandals. Ellen had made him look like a bimbo. Plus, he had a major problem with his penis. It was stubbornly erect. Women's panties are most definitely not made for men's genitals, he realised. The tiny panties struggled to hold the erection in. There was already a small bulge at the front of his skirt, luckily hidden between the folds of the pleats. He hoped it would stay that way.

"Amy."

Ms Ryder's voice from behind made him jump.

"I'd like you to remember the curtseying tonight, with Louise here. When you serve the food and such like. Proper curtsies tonight, not the little head nods you've been doing."

"Housemaids curtsey, Ms Ryder."

"Precisely, Amy. Make sure you do it. It doesn't have to be deep, but a small dip of one knee, the other leg behind ever so slightly. Take hold of your skirt hem with both hands. I think it would be most appropriate."

He gulped hard. "OK," he gasped.

His policy of appeasement was at the edge of its limits. Once he got through this dinner, he told himself it would all be over.

Fiona raised her eyebrows and waited. He didn't know what she wanted.

"A curtsey. Let me see how it looks."

Think of the bigger prize, he told himself. The job, the return to masculinity after this evening. Beating Ellen. He dipped his knee a couple of inches, one leg behind the other, the pink hem pinched out by a thumb and forefinger on each side.

His erection throbbed, it was uncomfortable stuffed into the small panties. The panties were tight across the centre of his balls, which had fallen out either side when he had dipped down for Fiona. This evening was going to be a challenge. He was relieved his penis remained held in. Just. He would need to be careful when he curtsied this evening if it wasn't to pop out.

Ms Ryder looked pleased with his effort at a curtsy and turned to leave. She then looked back. Her forehead creased for a moment.

"Your skirt's too short, Amy. It's not exactly evening dinner wear, is it."

It was the first time she had properly taken in what he was wearing. She leant forward, peering at his skirt.

"I can see the tops of your stockings."

"Ellen chose it, Ms Ryder. You told me I had to wear whatever she decided," he said brusquely. "I'll go and change." He failed to prevent an edge creeping into his voice.

Ms Ryder waved a hand airily.

"Not now, Amy, Louise'll be here in a moment. You look pretty." She scanned him up and down, her face showing disapproval. She bobbed her head to each side a couple of times in thought. "Never mind. You'll have to do."

David blushed deeply as she left. He lifted a leg and pushed a finger into his panties, tucking his balls back in. The doorbell rang. His stomach somersaulted, his throat closed. He breathed in deeply and opened the door.

A middle-aged woman bowled in as if she owned the place and dropped a small suitcase on the floor with a clunk. She held him in both arms, looked and kissed him on both cheeks. Her perfume smelled heavy and woody.

"You must be Amy, I'm so pleased to finally meet you, my dear. Fiona has told me all about you."

She let go, leant back and appraised him.

"Oh I say, you're not what I expected."

Her eyes ran over his too-blond hair and then across his skirt.

"Lovely legs. I'd die for legs like that, I really would, dearie"

She looked again and he wanted to run and hide.

"I suppose if I had your legs, I'd want to show them off with pretty little skirts too. Good for you, dear."

She suddenly placed both her hands inside his stocking tops. His brain stuttered for a short moment. She tugged at his stocking tops.

"What," was all he could exclaim as she pulled them up.

She stood back, then leant forward and whispered conspiratorially into my ear, "I could see the tops of your stockings. I think that's a little better, dearie. They're still showing but not quite so much. Looked a bit *tarty*, we wouldn't want that now, would we, dearie?"

Ms Ryder appeared in the hall. "Louise."

Louise marched over and they hugged a moment. They untangled.

"My, my, Fiona, you didn't tell me you had such a pretty little thing as an assistant."

Pretty little thing? David watched her in horror.

"I do think you need to help her out with her clothing, Fiona. It's rather revealing, I can see her panties."

Ms Ryder chuckled, took Louise Lipman's arm, and led her to the living room. She called back for David to bring them a glass of wine. He went to the kitchen. Ellen and Jenny were preparing the evening meal. Jenny seemed to be around more and more. They laughed together on seeing him.

He ignored them. They had won this little battle, but he was in it for the long game. This was a fight he was determined to win.

Chapter 27 — She Wants a Sissy Too

He went down on his haunches to choose a bottle of wine from the wine fridge. His erection screamed out from his tight panties. It showed as he knelt. He rearranged himself. He got up, opened the bottle, poured a measure in two wine glasses and took them into the living room. Louise and Ms Ryder were sitting in large black leather armchairs, at angles to each other. Between them was a small dark table. He placed the glasses on the table and stood back.

Ms Ryder rolled a finger in the air. It took a moment for him to understand what she wanted. He felt a little dizzy at the idea of a curtsey. He dipped a knee and held out his little skirt.

"Oh, how delightful," enthused Louise. "She's lovely. I want one like her."

His erection was as hard as ever. So hard, it was as if the skin might split with the intensity. Each humiliation ratcheted it up further. It was as if he was enjoying this humiliation. How could that be? He retreated to the kitchen. There was no respite there. Ellen and Jenny greeted him with laughter and conspiratorial whispers. He didn't know what they were giggling at initially.

They weren't looking at his face but somewhere lower down. He looked down and saw the reason for their amusement. His erection was pushing out the front of the little skirt, even through the folds in the pleats. Any hope of a shred of dignity was wiped away. It was obvious he was enjoying his debasement.

"Who's enjoying being a girly then? She loves being a girl." They said, now walking around him, circling like vultures.

Ellen lifted the front of his skirt. He tried to brush her hand away. It held firm against his. Their laughter raised. His erection was at right angles to his body, pushing the little patch of cotton out. Most of the panty was stretched away revealing a section of erect penis.

They left him; they had to return to the meal which was almost ready, cutting their fun for now. David sat down at the kitchen table and waited to be summoned to bring in the food. He had to share the room with these two women, his tormentors.

Ten minutes later, a bell tinkled from the dining room.

"That's Fiona. Take the starters in, girly." Ellen said, unable to resist a dig at any opportunity.

He jumped up and took the two plates she proffered him. He carried them through to the dining room where Fiona and Louise were now sitting. He placed the plates in front of the two ladies and stepped back. Fiona cleared her throat. She wanted a curtsy.

He held his skirt out and placed one leg behind and bent a knee. His erection raged and tingled. The feeling of needing to cum arrived without warning. He had had an erection for what seemed like the entire afternoon. This was dangerous, he realised. He would need to retreat to the bathroom or his bedroom to masturbate.

He needed to do the curtsey first. He straightened up and stood tall then dipped and held the tiny skirt hem out. His erection lost its fight to remain behind the sliver of cotton and fell out below the hem of his tiny skirt. He stood up sharply and it pointed out into the cool air, directly at an astonished Louise. His skirt was draped over it like a waiter's cloth over a wine bottle.

Louise Lipman's jaw fell, her eyes widened. He had a moment of feeling free and alive, his problems fading. A warm sensation went through his brain and shot down to his stomach and along the length of his straining erection. He discharged a thin spurt of gooey white fluid into the air. It lopped and dropped at Louise Lipman's feet, splashing across her shoes.

The feeling of warmth and pleasure dissipated in an instant. He went cold then hot. The room fell into silence. He pulled on his skirt and ran from the room and into the kitchen. He crashed into Jenny. He fell back on the floor, his legs open, his skirt up to his stomach. His reducing erection waving surrender in the warm kitchen air. A globule of semen dripped from the end in slow motion, running down the creased member and onto his balls.

Jenny and Ellen stared for a moment, eyes wide, then both squealed, their hands going to their faces. Fiona and Louise came in behind, he was still laying on the floor, legs wide apart like a plucked chicken. His penis lay flat against his body oozing cum.

"Amy. You will wipe Louise's shoes clean then go back into the dining room and clear up your mess. You will then go to your room." Fiona stared at him. "Get out of my sight."

David scrambled up. He flew to the cleaning cupboard and retrieved a cloth and cleaning spray. He scrambled back to Louise and knelt at her feet, He wiped his semen from her shoes. A feeling of nausea in his throat at what had happened. He thought he might be sick. Acidic bile came to his throat. He got up and shuffled back to the dining room and wiped the floor, cleaning up his mess. He returned to the kitchen.

"I'm sorry Ms Ryder, I'm sorry Ms Lipman. It was Ellen. She made me wear these ridiculous panties and this stupid skirt."

"Stop it." Fiona's face was dark and severe. "Ellen and Jenny did nothing apart from help you dress. Go. I don't want to see you again tonight."

"But, but, but Ms Ryder," he stuttered.

"Go. You're finished here, Amy. I don't want to see you again tonight."

Ms Ryder's lips were drawn tight. She waited a moment, recovering her temper.

"My office, first thing tomorrow." She pointed the way out of the kitchen.

David backed away towards the door. He saw Ellen with a lop-sided smile of satisfaction across her face. She had won. He turned and faced Louise who was in his path. Her eyebrows were raised and she had a wide smile slashed across her lips. Her eyes flitted down to his skirt and back up. He stopped for a moment, there was something in her eyes. It was not anger. There was something else. Amusement? He didn't know. He went around her and ran up the stairs and into his bedroom. He threw himself onto the bed, tears in his eyes. It had all gone horribly wrong. Ms Ryder's words were still ringing in his ears, *you're finished here, Amy.* Ellen had won. he had nothing and nowhere to go.

Chapter 28 — Curtsey Sissy

David stood outside Ms Ryder's closed office door the morning after last night's humiliation. He was dressed in the mid-thigh black skirt and plain blouse, thankful he would never have to wear the dreadful clothes from last night again. This would be the last time he would have to wear a skirt again. Good, he thought. *Maybe?*

He heard Ms Ryder moving around behind the door. A mild breeze blew around his skirt from the kitchen. The back door must be open, he guessed Ellen was about.

A gentle throat-clearing cough came from behind him. Louise was leaning against the kitchen door frame, a cup of steaming coffee in one hand. She had one leg across the other. Her hair was down, big brown and tussled in a 1980s way. She had a knee-length skirt on.

"Good morning, Amy," she said.

He swallowed hard, he felt his face burn red. "Good morning, Ms Lipman." He couldn't decide whether to curtsy or not. An apology would be better. "I'm so sorry for what happened last night. I can't explain. I didn't want to wear those clothes. They made me. It was...." He trailed off. It was useless.

Louise studied him a moment. "Maybe best if you didn't curtsy this morning, dearie. Not after what happened last night." Amusement danced in her eyes.

He looked down at the floor, his face burning puce with embarrassment. She didn't appear annoyed.

"Good luck with Fiona," she said. "I believe you'll find she's calmed down now." She said. "I've had a word with her. I think you'll find things a little smoother. A little different?"

He didn't know what she meant. It was as if she had found last night's humiliation funny. He turned back to Fiona's office door and knocked. Fiona called out to enter. He twisted the handle and entered. He glanced at Ms Ryder at her desk, then looked down at the floor. She told him to close the door and to come over and stand by her side. He did as instructed and waited for the sword to fall on him and his job.

Ms Ryder breathed deeply. It was coming. He would be kicked out, no job, no home. No male clothes. Despite Louise Lipman's reassuring words, it was over. Ellen had won.

"Well," she started. "That was quite a show last night, wasn't it?"

He held his hands in front of his black skirt. More modest than last night. No danger of the same problem of the escaping erection occurring this morning. He would miss wearing a skirt, the sensations of the soft material wafting around his smooth legs. But, it couldn't last, that phase was over.

"Yes, Ms Ryder. I'm sorry."

He felt her looking him over as he continued to stare hard at the floor. *Get it over with,* he thought. *Say you're disappointed in last night's behaviour and send me back to London.* Even though he did not think it was his fault, it was Ellen's. And she, Ellen, had won.

"Amy. I don't appreciate seeing an erect penis pointed at me from three feet away as I'm about to eat." She shuddered exaggeratedly. "And worse. I don't appreciate you then ejaculating. Disgusting."

He waited for the words to come, *I'm terminating your employment. Gross misconduct. Flashing an erection at me and my agent at the dinner table. Then cumming over her feet.*

"I understand, Ms Ryder." What else could he say?

She waved a hand as if to say, don't bother.

"So I'm removing you from the position of personal assistant. I'm making it a shared role between Ellen and Jenny. Ellen for the more complex things and Jenny for the easier tasks. She's young. Maybe she'll grow into it in time."

His entire body slumped. It was no surprise. It was over. Ellen had got exactly what she wanted. A complete victory.

"However."

Her word hung in the air. *However? There was something else?*

"Louise spoke with me about what happened. After we'd finished last night." Fiona looked around the room, searching for the words.

He wanted to say *and*.

"It seems she wasn't at all upset at your little show. On the contrary. She found the whole event and the great unveiling of you as a male underneath all that girly top layer, most amusing. You had her fooled. She was enthused.

We had quite a chat about it. And, in the end, a laugh over a brandy or two."

This wasn't what he had been expecting.

"Louise thinks there are lots of benefits to having a submissive sissy in one's service. She told us she has some experience of this." Ms Ryder raised her eyebrows. "Apparently, feminised men make excellent submissive servants for some reason, according to Louise anyway." She looked up in thought. "Who would have guessed?" She continued in deep thought for a moment digesting what she had said.

Submissive? Servant? Feminised men? David had no idea where this was going and waited for her to come to the point.

"There's been another development which affects what I'm about to say. The virus lockdown has deepened and the police now have a presence in the village. They are stopping any movement. You can't leave, even if I wanted to kick you out. So I have to think about what I'm going to do with you. In the short term for sure."

He wondered if he had been reprieved. Maybe, but he guessed there would be a price to pay from what she had said.

"This also means Louise can't leave either. So she'll be staying here too. There's plenty of room. She was really on your side about the events last night."

His body perked up at her words.

"So this is what we've decided. It's an offer, if you like." Ms Ryder thought a moment, as if choosing her words carefully.

He was impatient, desperate to hear what she was going to offer him.

"Louise wants you to remain as you are."

He didn't understand. "What does that mean, Ms Ryder? I remain as your assistant?"

A thin smile crept over her face. "Not exactly, Amy. Louise wants you to remain as a girl. As a sissy, as she calls it. She wants you to become more feminine. Your job will become more of a.." she thought hard. "More of a housemaid. Serving, cleaning. Leaving Ellen and Jenny with the more important things to do associated with my job."

He couldn't believe what he was hearing. More feminine? What kind of choice was this? Remain as a girl? His mind raced, he mumbled about needing to think about it. He had to give himself time to think. He needed the work but he couldn't continue as a girl, it was wrong. What should he do?

"Louise was rather taken with you. She hadn't spotted you as a male. Until your thingy popped out and you made a mess on her shoes." She allowed herself a small laugh at the memory. "She thinks you have more potential as a maid. A housemaid. Useless as a personal assistant, as we saw."

The office door opened. Louise strode in as if she owned the place. "Is she going to be our little sissy girly? I hope so, I have so many ideas. It's been a while since I trained a sissy maid."

He looked on in horror. "I don't have a choice, do I?"

Louise clapped her hands in glee. "No you don't and that's how I like it."

"Yes, Ms Lipman," he said. He saw she was going to be more demanding than Ms Ryder.

"And Amy?" Louise said.

"Yes, Ms Lipman."

"You will address me as Mistress, OK?"

He didn't see the harm if that's what turned her on.

"Yes, Mistress."

Ms Lipman's face lit up. "Good sissy. We're going to have such fun with you, Amy. Me, Fiona here, Ellen and Jenny."

"Ellen and Jenny?" He asked surprised.

"Well yes, Amy, them too. How wonderful." She turned to Fiona."Show him what he's going to be wearing." Louise's enthusiasm for this project spilled into her face and eyes.

Fiona typed into her laptop. She waited for a site to load. She twisted the screen around to face him. He peered into the images.

Louise's voice came from behind him. "I'm going to put you in a cock cage and a butt plug, like you can see on the screen. Or in your case, a clitty cage and vagina plug." She laughed to herself at her joke. "After your little show, it's obvious you need to be controlled. I'm going to order them online and they should be here next week." She let this sink in. "Show him his new clothing Fiona."

Fiona typed in something and another site popped up. Images of models in little frilly maid dresses, tiny aprons, vertiginous heels, fish-net stockings, pink bows in blond hair.

His eyes widened. "Surely not." His voice tapered away.

"Yes surely," Louise continued for him. "These will be your work clothes. I'm placing an order for several dresses, stockings and shoes for you. You need to look the part, Amy. But don't worry, we'll be teaching you how to be a good sissy-maid." She went over to stand next to Ms Ryder. "And if you're a good girl, then there's a whole lot more we can offer you." She thought for a moment. "No. Offer isn't the right word. It won't be your choice. I'm going to mould you into what you should be."

He gulped. That was not good. These things looked uncomfortable. But here he had a job, home, food and comfort. And there was that tingle in his penis at the sight of the images on the screen.

His life was about to get even more complicated. And much, much more girly.

THE END of BOOK 1

Continue reading for a sneak preview of Lockdown Feminization Book 2.

Chapter 1

The dress did not cover his panties. It was bright pink with white petticoats and flared out like a ballerina's tutu. He was relieved that he was permitted panties, even though the harsh outline of his metal cock cage was clearly visible through them.

He walked to his full-length mirror hanging on the back of his bedroom door. Walked was not really the correct verb. Small steps in four-inch heels meant he was moving across the room on tip-toes. His shoes were padlocked to his ankles, much like his cock cage was locked to his penis and balls.

He had to ensure he was perfectly presented before returning downstairs to serve the four ladies living there afternoon tea. Mistress Lipman would punish him for the slightest error, however small. It was as if she enjoyed spanking him in front of the other ladies. Panties down, over her knee. Sometimes with her hand, other times with a wooden spoon.

He looked in closely at his face. Bright red lipstick, freshly applied, no smudges: check. Hair light blond, thick and wavy, no grey roots: check. Pink bow tied at the back of his hair, large and extravagant, both bows exactly six inches diameter: check, she would measure them. False eyelashes, attached: check. Large looped earrings clipped on: check. He inspected his hands. Long false nails, pink, glossy, no chipped ends, none loose: check.

He turned his back to the mirror and looked over the puffy shoulders of his dress. Seams straight on the black fish-net stockings: check. He turned back. False boobs level under the bra: check.

He was ready. He made for the top stair and steadied himself on the bannister. It was tricky getting down on four-inch stilettos. He heard the bell tinkling from below, the mistresses were getting impatient, he was taking too long. This could only mean one thing. Punishment.

David Amey's forced feminisation into the sissy Amy gets a whole lot more intense in Lockdown Feminization 2

I do hope you enjoyed Lockdown Feminization 1.

If so, please leave me a review.

Lady Alexa
xxx

Don't forget to follow my real-life Forced Feminization and Female

Led Relationship blog at *www.ladyalexauk.com*

Printed in Great Britain
by Amazon